The Tip-Off

A Smart Jocks Novel

REBECCA JENSHAK

The Tip-Off

Also by Rebecca Jenshak

"Kisses are a better fate than wisdom."
-EE Cummings

one

Zeke

*W*atching a grown man intentionally lose a game of PIG is downright embarrassing. The things people do for love.

I shake my head at Wes as I rebound the basketball from his weak shot attempt. The odds of him missing three in a row are as bad as my own and I could have made any one of those shots blindfolded.

I gotta hand it to him, though, he's a pretty good actor and his girlfriend is eating it up.

"That's G for you. I win!" Blair squeals and jumps up and down in front of my buddy, her ponytail swinging wildly like a whip. I toss her the ball and she brings it up over her head in victory and turns in a circle calling out to me and the rest of my roommates who are hanging around our half-court gym. "Reigning PIG champion, folks. You don't want any of this."

I chuckle and she steps toward me. "Come on, big guy. Let's see what the number one NBA draft picks got."

"Projected. He hasn't been drafted yet." Wes wraps both arms around his girl and tugs her to him.

"Thanks for the vote of confidence," I tell him dryly.

"Just want to make sure you don't start slacking, letting the media's hard-on for you go to your head."

I resist the urge to continue our banter by telling him to fuck off since Blair is present. My mom would lose her shit if she knew I was dropping F-bombs in front of girls. Besides, I know that underneath the jokes, no one has my back like Wes does.

"Let's go, senorita," Joel draws out the word, exaggerating the pronunciation as he pulls his shirt over his head and tosses it out of bounds.

"What'd I tell you about using the Spanish on my girlfriend?" Wes asks, not letting go of Blair.

Nathan sets his beer next to Joel's shirt and pushes him out of the way. "I got this. I'm three beers in and unbeatable."

It's a rare weeknight that we're all home at the same time. Since the season ended, we've each fallen into our own routines. Wes spending more time with Blair, Joel spending more time with his girlfriend Katrina, and Nathan doing whatever it is Nathan does. I've been right here making sure I do everything I can to get that top pick Wes is ragging me about.

In less than two months Wes and I will be graduating. He's staying in Valley as the team's newest assistant coach, so it's really just me that's leaving, and man that feels weird. Exciting too, though. I don't know where I'm going yet. East Coast, West Coast, Midwest. Honestly, I don't care so long as I can keep playing ball.

"Actually, I'm gonna have to take a raincheck." Blair bounces the ball to Nathan. "Vanessa and Gabby should be here any minute to pick me up for girls' night." She turns in Wes' arms and they get tangled up kissing and groping like she won't be back later tonight. She sleeps over every night.

My buddy has it bad and I'm happy for him. Blair's a solid chick.

"Speaking of," Nathan says and nods to the door as Gabby and Vanessa enter.

Joel and I hang back as everyone else walks over to greet them. I watch Gabby smile and hug Blair and then Nathan. She just moved to Valley, but she and Blair went to high school together and have remained tight, so she's quickly becoming a regular face at the house.

Her long blonde hair is down, and she keeps her chin tilted down ever-so-slightly so the long strands fall into her face. Her gaze meets mine over Nathan's shoulder and I hold my breath. I don't know what it is about her, but when she's in the room, my palms tingle with anticipation like I'm about to walk out on the floor before a game.

Completely unaware, Joel dribbles in front of me blocking my view of Gabby. I step to the side, but she's not looking at me anymore. "Hey, man, you busy tomorrow night?"

"No, I don't think so. Why?"

"Blair wants to have a party for Gabby. Thought we'd take it one step further and throw a surprise party for all the girls. One last big hurrah. You in?"

"Sounds good," I say absently and turn to the basket and shoot a jumper.

"I'm not even gonna tell Wes until tomorrow so there's less of a chance he slips and tells Blair."

"Good call." I glance back like I'm looking at the happy couple, but they're not who my eyes settle on.

"You and Wes are going to ride over and pick us up. The girls and I'll be at the theater for Katrina's play. Then we'll ride back to the house together. Cool?"

"I guess so." I dribble the ball and watch Gabby talk animatedly to the group – eyes bright and hands waving in the air.

Joel takes two steps backward to the door. "I'm heading to Katrina's. Don't forget about tomorrow. Oh, and wear something nice. The limo will be downstairs at eight o'clock. Be there or be lame."

"The limo?"

"Yeah, we're doing it up right. Classy as fuck." He winks and jogs backward a few more steps before turning.

Everyone leaves at once and the only one who offers me a goodbye glance is Gabby. She lifts one hand in a small wave, but my response is so delayed that by the time I get my hand in the air to wave back, she's gone.

With the gym to myself, I lift the headphones from around my neck and settle them on my ears, rack the extra balls, and start my routine. I've just finished my ball-handling warmup and am starting in on my shooting drills when Wes returns. I drop my headphones back to my neck.

"Are you getting in another workout?" he asks as he

walks over to the rack.

"Nah, not really, just thought I'd get my shots in and kill some time until I can eat my last meal of the day."

He picks up a ball and smirks. "Sara still have you on that cutting diet?"

"Yes," I grumble.

My agent wants me to lean out before I start interviewing with NBA teams. I'm bigger than the average center, and though it hasn't been a problem up to this point, I don't want there to be any question, any slightest of reservations, about drafting me. If dropping weight proves that, so be it.

"How about a little one on one, for old time's sake?"

"Think you still got it? I just watched a girl with very little athletic ability – no offense to Blair – destroy you at PIG."

He smirks but doesn't answer as he moves to the top of the key and checks the ball. Wes and I played together for four years until an injury ended his college career. The boot he had to wear during recovery is newly off, but I'm not about to take it easy on him. Unlike him, I don't throw competition in the name of love or friendship.

Wes dribbles the ball, a cocky grin on his face. I know his moves as well as my own, so I'm prepared when he pulls a crossover. If I were anyone else, he'd be putting me on skates right now, but I hang with him all the way to the basket. He's forced to shoot around me but gets lucky with an off-balance jumper.

"Check," I say after I've rebounded the ball and taken it to the three-point line. I narrow my gaze on his and give him my best intimidating smirk. "I think you got slower."

He shakes his head. "Your smack talk won't work on me, Z."

"We'll see," is all I say before I crab dribble, backing him up with my large frame. The determination to show me he's still got it is written all over his face. And he does, but I'm still better. He's playing me close, chest pressed to my back to keep me from drop stepping low – my favorite move. Favorite, but not only. I go high and use my height and long arms to get a hook shot off and in.

"You've gotten even better," he says as he walks the ball to the three-point line. "Either that or I really have gotten slower. How many shots are you getting in a day?"

I shrug. "Six hundred or so."

Wes looks at me like I'm nuts, but lots of guys swear by shooting five hundred plus shots a day. Steph Curry and Kobe Bryant are just two in a long line of successful guys doing it. Next level skill and talent are earned with a lot of repetition and focus. It's the price of success and I'll pay it every day until I make it.

The next night at eight o'clock on the dot, I head downstairs feeling uneasy. Parties aren't generally my thing, but it's not that alone that has me unbuttoning my sleeves and rolling them up to get some air. Something about the plan for the night just doesn't sit right. A surprise party? A limo? What the hell have I gotten myself into?

Wes is already waiting in the living room and he shoves a clear box in my direction. There's some sort of flower inside.

"What's this?" I ask, noticing he has two other identical boxes in his left hand.

"It's a corsage." He watches my face for understanding. "It's for Gabby."

"What does she do with it?"

"You've never given a girl a corsage before?"

"I can't give her this." I try and push it back into his hand, but he won't take it.

"You have to. She can't be the only girl that doesn't get one. That's shitty. Besides, she's basically your date."

"What do you mean she's basically my date?"

Wes' phone beeps and he looks down at the screen. "Limo's here."

"Hold up," I say before he can open the door. "Explain."

Wes snorts and looks at me like I'm clueless. I guess I am. "Me and Blair, Joel and Katrina, Vanessa and Mario…" His voice trails off, allowing me to fill in the rest.

"What about Nathan? Where is he and why can't he give this… thing to her." I shake the box in my hand.

"Nathan's staying to get the party going. Would you rather stay here and play hostess or stand next to a pretty girl all night?"

He opens the door and I follow.

"That's what I thought."

Vanessa steps out of the limo. "Hello, boys." She

gives us both a once over before nodding her approval. Vanessa, Blair, and Gabby are like the three amigos lately, so I'm surprised to see her without them.

"What are you doing here?" Wes asks. "I thought we were surprising you?"

"Surprising me?" She shakes her head. "Who do you think helped Joel put this together? I mean, honestly, like he was going to leave you two unsupervised to pull this off."

"Fair enough." Wes chuckles, steps past her and slides into the limo. I try to do the same, but Vanessa moves with me.

"Hello, Zeke," she says. "You clean up nice. I almost didn't recognize you without your headphones."

"Thanks, Vanessa. You look nice too."

"Let's talk strategy. This is going to be the best surprise party ever." She claps her hands and then climbs into the vehicle.

Strategy?

Once we're all in the limo, Vanessa's boyfriend Mario offers us a beer and a knowing look as Vanessa gets right to it. "Blair, Gabby, and Joel are all at the theater for Katrina's play. Joel's going to come out to get you two and you're going to storm in there looking all handsome and surprise the girls." She pulls out a rolled-up poster board and hands it to me. "When they see you, hold this up."

As I unroll it, glitter explodes. So does my head when I read what it says. *Go to Prom with us?* is written in big sparkly letters.

"Prom?" I'm not sure if I'm more thrown by the high school throwback or that this whole thing has been orchestrated as a big group date. Fuck, it's warm in here. I pull at the collar on my shirt. I'm going to kill Joel for leaving out some very important details.

Wes covers a laugh with his fist. "Uh, yeah, that's the other thing. Gabby and Katrina missed their high school proms so that's where the limo and corsages come into play. It's a surprise party with a prom vibe." He claps me on the shoulder and shrugs. A shrug that tells me he'd do anything for Blair and by extension, Gabby. "It's gonna be fun."

two

Gabby

THIS is why girls go to the bathroom together. So they can talk about boys, borrow lipstick, *and* so they don't get lost.

I push through the crowd careening my neck left and then right and walking on my tiptoes to try and see through the mass of people. There are a lot of great things about being short... not being able to see over tall people isn't one of them.

Relief washes over me when I spot my friends across the large lobby of the Valley campus theater. The front doors are open and the breeze filters through, bringing with it the sweet smell of spring. It's a beautiful night to be out, and though this is my first time watching a campus performance, I suspect the weather is partly responsible for everyone lingering after the show.

"I made it." I let out a long breath as I join Blair and Katrina.

"You got lost again, didn't you?" Blair asks with a teasing smile. Damn best friends, they always call you out.

"Not lost," I insist. "Delayed. There was a long line for the ladies and then I had to weave through a million people to find you. It's like a Beyoncé concert up in here."

"It's one of the best turnouts I've ever seen, and the show was fantastic."

At Blair's praise, Katrina blushes. Tonight's play was written entirely by her and all the actors were students too.

"It really was amazing. Congratulations."

"Thanks." She lets her shoulders droop. "I'm so glad it's over."

"We should celebrate."

No sooner than Blair says the words I spot Joel, Wes, and Zeke walking toward us with swagger that splits the room to let them through.

"I think Joel has something planned. He was being weird earlier when I asked what the plan was for tonight."

My throat is dry, and I have to clear it twice so my voice is more than a whisper. "Uh, guys."

I nudge Blair and she follows my gaze to the guys.

Going to college via online classes has one big disadvantage – no boys. No running into a handsome guy at a frat party – how Vanessa met Mario. No looking across the classroom and enjoying the eye candy – like Blair and Wes. And no running into your soul mate in

University Hall like Joel and Katrina.

The whole soulmate thing I don't care about so much, but I am looking forward to the eye candy, and the three in front of me are some of the very best examples of why I decided to finally move to Valley for my senior year. The spring semester isn't quite over, but I thought I would feel less like a freshman if I got to know some people before Fall classes start. The next few months are my own version of orientation. Though the agenda is more social than academic.

My gaze flits over each of them. From Wes' blue eyes and crooked smile to Joel's jet-black hair and charm to Zeke's dark skin and large build... good God, my body shivers with appreciation as I get a good look at him.

Zeke Sweets, basketball king and NBA prospect, has traded his jersey for grey slacks and a black button-down shirt. My eyes trace the ink running up his left hand and disappearing into the rolled sleeve of his dress shirt. It's only when I'm giving that muscular arm a second sweep that I notice the paper in one hand and the clear box in the other.

He shifts the clear box awkwardly, so it's lodged between his side and elbow and unrolls the paper. It says something, but between the fluorescent lights bouncing off the glitter and the way Zeke's brown eyes lock on mine, I'm having a hard time reading it.

"What's going on?" Blair asks.

Joel responds for the guys by stepping forward, tossing me a wink, and handing Katrina a clear box identical to the one Zeke has. "Prom do-over, babydoll."

It's then that Wes nudges Zeke forward and the

mystery box is pushed out in front of me. I giggle at the large corsage inside, a nervous reaction. A peek at Blair beside me confirms she had something to do with this. I missed my high school prom and it's never sat right with her. In all honesty, I'm more excited about starting over than trying to make up for the past, but I appreciate the thought.

With shaky hands, I take the box and Zeke looks like I've taken the weight of the world off his shoulders. "Wanna go to prom with me?" he asks with just enough humor in his tone that I think he might find this as ridiculous as me.

"Love to."

Turns out this prom is better than whatever I missed in high school. The back yard of The White House, the nickname for the mansion Zeke, Wes, Joel, and Nathan live in, is packed. A DJ booth is set up in one corner with large speakers that vibrate my insides as we pass by it. Bodies push and grind to an old jam and I raise my arms with the rest of the crowd when Busta tells us to put our hands where his eyes could see.

"This playlist is killer," I yell over the music to Blair. "Way better than whatever you had at your prom. And I cannot believe you guys got a foam machine." On the other side of the party, people are disappearing into the foam and reemerging with big smiles.

"You said you always wanted to go to a foam party,

now you have."

I throw my arms around her neck. "You are amazing."

"I can't take credit for this. I had a small idea for a party and Joel took it to a whole other level."

We find a spot somewhere in the middle of the party and set up in a circle – girls on the inside and guys hanging back. Wes stands two steps behind Blair, beer in hand. He's not dancing but doing a tiny little head bob to the music.

Vanessa has a similar setup – although V is turned toward her boyfriend Mario making it very clear she's dancing just for him.

Joel and Katrina have disappeared altogether, but that's not unusual for them. I think they spend more time naked than clothed when they have a night without Katrina's son Christian.

The sight of Mario and Wes watching their girls so possessive and adoringly makes me happy. But also, insanely jealous like if they weren't already my friends, I'd hate them for being so ridiculously in love.

In beat to the song, I turn to the side so I can see Zeke standing behind me. He's not looking at me possessively or adoringly. Actually, he's not looking at me at all.

What does it take to get Zeke Sweets' attention? Basketballs for boobs? And I don't mean huge boobs, I mean literal basketballs. The only time I've really seen him smile is when he's on the basketball court.

We've barely spoken to each other since getting in the limo to drive to the party, but I can't help but feel a little burst of pride being here with him. He's so handsome and big and strong and intense and handsome and… did I already mention handsome?

"Gabby baby!" Nathan shouts as he enters our couple circle. He tucks one side of his long hair behind an ear and then tackle hugs me.

I let out a surprised chuckle as all the wind is knocked out of me. "Good to see you, too."

Nathan and I have become friends in my short time at Valley, which is nice because I anticipate I'll be spending a lot of time at The White House since my best friends are dating jocks.

With a hand around my waist, Nathan moves us with the beat. The beer he's holding in one hand spills onto my arm and he backs up as he apologizes and then his gaze falls to my dress like he's just now seeing my outfit.

"Wow, Gabby. You trying to kill me in that dress?"

His words make me smile, but I swat playfully at him dodging the compliment like a boss.

Vanessa twirls, raises her hands, and yells, "Let's move up closer to the foam."

I nod and Nathan and I follow behind her. I peek over my shoulder to see if Z is following and he is, though unhurried and not all that enthusiastically. We're a train moving through the crowd. Mario holding onto Vanessa, me with a hand on V's back so no one can separate us and holding my other hand behind me grasping Blair's. Nathan is beside me and I don't look back again to verify but I assume Wes is back there pulling up the rear with Zeke.

Every step closer to the crowd dancing in the cloud-like substance makes my heart thump wilder in my chest. Now this is a party! It's not as packed in the foam, most people are staying on the outskirts of it, but I want in.

"I think this is as far as I go," Vanessa says and Blair nods in agreement.

"Sorry, Gabby, that foam freaks me out a bit," Nathan adds.

I mock pout but no one steps forward.

Wes shoves Zeke forward and my date's eyes widen in panic. The nice thing to do would be to let him off the hook, but my desire to get him to dance with me outweighs every nice bone in my body. Also, I find Zeke's presence a comfort, like I can be as crazy and reckless as I want, and he'll keep me safe. Stupid, I know, considering we've barely spoken. But if it came to blows, I think he'd at least step in front of me and block me with his giant frame.

"Let's go, big guy." I grab his hand and pull. He budges without me really having to put any weight behind it and we enter the foam, leaving our traitorous friends behind and joining a group of girls who look to be as excited as I feel.

They welcome us, widening the circle before getting lost to the music again. I do the same with Zeke standing behind me. He's closer now than before and maybe it's the foam or the way no one is watching us in here, but I grow bolder. I turn and place my hands on his chest, moving with the beat. I keep my eyes downcast until one of his hands finds my hip. My breath hitches and I move an inch closer and meet his gaze.

Zeke's eyes are a light brown, warm and soulful, and right now they're finally on me. Wow. The force of a thousand suns. All that intensity focused on me, I was not prepared for it. I reach down to the foam at my feet and scoop up a handful, stand, and blow it into his face. It takes him a moment to react, but slowly a smile spreads on his face and then he shocks me by reciprocating – tossing giant handfuls of foam at me, hurling it so fast and furious there's a cloud around us. I swat at the foam until I can see his smiling face and giggle, look down, and prepare to make another move.

He holds his hand up and says, "Truce."

"Okay," I say at the same time I move to grab for more, but he's quick and catches my wrist. His large fingers burn into my skin and he shakes his head, still smiling.

The foam builds between us and his touch disappears from my wrist only to be replaced by his fingertips brushing against the side of my face and pushing the foam away. It lasts only a second, but I feel it even after he's dropped his hand back to his side.

The song changes and the girls in the foam with us squeal in delight as the opening to Lizzo's "Truth Hurts" begins to play.

I feel on top of the world as I give myself over to the beat like I've only done in my bedroom for the past three years. Zeke doesn't exactly dance, but he seems more relaxed now and I'm patting myself on the back for pulling him in here. All he needed was a little forced fun.

One song turns to five and I'm drenched with a combination of foam and sweat when I turn back to face the middle of the circle. I offer a shy smile to the girl to my left. She returns it and then tilts her head and studies me. "You've got something…" She takes a step toward me, smooths a hand over her face at the same time she must realize the only thing on my face is… my face.

My scarred face.

Stupid. Stupid. Stupid, Gabby.

My hand flies to the left side of my face and I give her a reassuring smile. After all, it's not her fault.

They can make mascara that withstands a good cry fest, but so far, I haven't found a foundation that is as magical. Which means mine is gone with the foam and the lines on my face are more visible. The scars on my face from a car accident my senior year of high school are never completely hidden, but with several layers of concealer, foundation, and setting spray, it's not usually obvious enough that people gasp in horror – yep, that's happened.

"Sorry," she says and averts her eyes back to the middle of the circle.

I don't look around to the other girls. One thing I hate more than gawking – the pity. As if my life were defined by my face. As if I'm somehow less than because I'm not perfect. As if they're better than me because they wear their scars on the inside. And I flipping hate that I feel like they might be right.

I turn to face my date and hope he'll shield me from this awkward, awful moment or maybe whisk me away and tell me I'm beautiful no matter what. Cheesy, right? But I long to hear those words from someone even if it's not true.

Zeke's eyes are warm and understanding as his gaze drops to the scars on my face and then to the girls dancing around us. "Wanna head back?"

Well, it's not a profession of beauty or love, but it's

an excuse out of here anyway. I grab his arm and duck behind him. With as much dignity as I can muster, I shimmy out of that foam like my pride didn't wash away with my makeup.

Man, I was stoked about a real-life foam party. I forgot one minor detail. Foam is made of water.

three

Gabby

*Z*eke leads me into the gym on the second story of The White House.

"When I said I wanted to go somewhere quiet, this isn't exactly what I had in mind."

"It's the only place off limits during parties."

He turns on the lights and grabs two basketballs from a rack. He extends one to me and I eye it curiously. He can't be serious.

"Really?"

He looks unsure as he gives a little shrug, ball still held out toward me. His eyes light up and he drops the ball to my feet. "Wait, I know what we need."

Confused but intrigued, I watch as he tucks the other basketball under his arm and takes out his phone. His head bounces from side to side as his thumbs tap on the screen.

"Here we go," he says as music pumps into the room. He pockets his phone and dribbles toward the basket.

I take a moment to look around the room, taking in the gym. I've seen it before, but never really appreciated how nice it is. The polished wood floor is a half-court version of the one at Ray Fieldhouse from the blue and yellow lines on the court to the Ray Roadrunner mascot painted on the wall. It's a sweet place. Joel's dad is the president of Valley U and he bought this place and outfitted it with everything the guys could possibly need – and way more. It's not as outrageous as some of the big university athletic dorms, but it's pretty over the top.

Moving up to the free throw line, I try to think back on what I learned in junior high basketball while I watch Zeke take shots. He's more relaxed than I've seen him all night. Even in dress clothes, he looks like he belongs with a basketball in his hands.

"It's a little intimidating shooting hoops with you."

"Don't worry about it, I make everyone look bad on the court."

I'm taken back by his words until I meet his gaze. He's smiling and wears a cocky grin he's never flashed my direction before. I feel that look in my toes. "You've got jokes, huh?"

He shoots, rebounds his ball and then dribbles to me. "Let's see what you got."

Under his scrutiny, I take my time getting into position at the free throw line and then shoot. I cringe as the ball doesn't quite make it to the rim. Airball.

Zeke gets my ball and brings it back to me. "Try again."

"Who knew the night could get more humiliating," I mutter under my breath, but I take another shot anyway. This one at least hits the rim.

After my fourth miss, he hands me the ball and then instructs me to widen my stance. "Good, now bring your right foot forward just a tiny bit."

Instead of trying to talk me through the upper body, he guides my arms up and into position and then moves my hands where he wants them. Goosebumps race to the surface at his warm touch. His hands are strong and steady, and it's a sad realization that this is the most a man has touched me since my car accident nearly four years ago.

"Alright, use your legs and really follow it through, let it roll off those fingertips."

With more concentration and focus than I've used since trying to read through Game of Thrones fan theories, I stare down the red rim and shoot.

"Yes!" I jump as the ball goes through the net. Freaking finally.

"There you go. Nice. Do it again." He sends the ball back to me with a bounce pass.

Intent brown eyes watch me as I line up and try and get into the same position.

"So, I've gathered parties aren't really your thing. Is this where you usually hide out?"

"Who says I usually hide out?"

"Everyone. Also, I was in town visiting Blair for the party after the last home game of the season. I don't remember seeing you."

"It's not that they aren't my *thing*, I just don't party much during the season. What about you?"

"Are parties my thing?"

He nods.

"Yes. Well, I want them to be. I've only been to the one and I wasn't a student yet. So, this is my first official college party. I'm officially a fan, though. There's something so magical about the bass of the music and people dancing and having a good time. Well, everyone but you."

"I'm having a fine time."

"Wow, you really know how to make a girl feel special. You're having a *fine* time. At least I don't have to worry about you telling anyone how awful our date was."

"Why's that?"

"Because you don't talk much."

"Burn," he says and his lips curve into another smile. "I'm a man of few words." Palming the ball in one hand, he raises it toward me like he's pointing. "How about the best date I've been on in four years?"

"Well, then you'd just be lying."

He raises a brow and then turns to shoot without speaking.

I dribble and bring the ball up, pausing before I send the ball sailing to the basket. "This is the only date you've been on since then, isn't it?"

I remember the guys giving him shit once about never dating, but I'd assumed they were exaggerating the situation.

He winks and keeps rebounding his ball and putting it back. He's gotten into it now and is shooting like he's at practice. Basketball in dress clothes – it's a good look.

"So, parties aren't your thing, dating isn't your thing,

what is your thing?" He opens his mouth to tell me what I already know, but I stop him. "Besides basketball."

He shakes his head. "It's my only thing."

"If you had to give up food or basketball, which would you choose?"

He dribbles as he answers. "I'd die without food."

"Some things are worth dying for."

A deep chuckle echoes in the gym. "So, basketball for three weeks… maybe less since I'll be wasting away or a lifetime without it?"

"Mhmmm."

"That's savage."

"That's what makes it such a good question. You can learn a lot about a person by what they're willing to give up for the things they really love."

He agrees with a head bob and another quiet chuckle and goes back to focusing on the basketball goal.

"Peanut butter or jelly?"

"Both."

"That's cheating. You can only pick one."

"Peanut butter."

"Show up to class naked or knee to the balls?"

"Class naked." He shivers like the other option is too awful to contemplate.

I keep firing off questions and he answers – not in a lot of words, but I'm getting used to the subtle way his body language says what he doesn't. Right now, he's relaxed, and he thinks I'm at least a little bit funny. I can work with that.

I give up shooting and sit on the floor, ball in my lap, as I watch him. He's really something to take in. I've seen him play before, of course, but up close, all that testosterone and skill is just... well, it's a little breathtaking if I'm honest. This is almost better than the party.

As if he can read my thoughts, he looks over and stares at me a beat, sympathy in the way he takes me in. "Do you want to go back out to the party?"

I look toward the door with longing but shake my head. "I don't think so. Tonight is kind of a bust. This is not how I pictured it going down." Guilt steals the air from my lungs, and it burns as I let out a breath. "Please don't tell anyone I said that. Blair would be devastated if she thought I didn't have a good time tonight."

Zeke places the ball on the floor beside me and sits on it. "I won't say a word."

Now that I believe.

"What would you give up food for?"

I think for a minute. "I don't know. I don't have one big thing I want like you do. I want to do it all now that I'm at Valley, all the normal college things. That probably sounds dumb to the guy who is about to graduate and get drafted into the NBA."

"Not dumb at all. Certainly not any dumber than choosing a death sentence so I can play basketball for three weeks. Shit, I would probably be awful too without any food to give me energy." He looks really bothered by this, more so than the fact he'd literally be starving to death.

I laugh softly. "That is pretty dumb."

"Got anything specific in mind or are you just winging it?"

I've had a lot of time to think about this, so I nod. "I have a few things in mind."

He waits for me to continue, but I redirect instead. "Does no dating mean no anything? No kissing, no…" I'm a twenty-one-year-old woman, but I can't bring myself to say the word.

Thankfully he knows where I'm going. "I've hooked up occasionally, but it's hard—"

"I'll bet." I slap my hand over my mouth. "Oh God, I'm sorry, I didn't mean to say that out loud." I keep my head buried and wave him on. "Please continue."

Humor laces his tone, but the words are serious. "Dividing attention between two things like that… it stops you from being great at either one."

"Lots of professional athletes are married."

"Yeah and there's like an eighty percent divorce rate among them, too."

I start to laugh but realize he's completely serious. "What about casual relationships?"

He shrugs. "It's still a distraction."

I don't know why this hurts my feelings, but my face heats with rejection, which doesn't make any sense. We're on a date. He asked me to be his date. The man gave me a freaking corsage.

"If you haven't been on a date in…"

"Four years," he supplies as he stands and moves toward the basket. "Maybe five."

"Why tonight? I mean, obviously I'm amazing, but that's quite a streak to break for a girl you barely know."

He glances back and the panic in his eyes tells me everything. How did I not put it together before?

"Oh God." I cover my face with both hands as my emotions spiral. "Blair and Wes put you up to this, didn't they?" The words come out jumbled through my hands, but when he sighs, I feel confident he heard me. Of course, our best friends orchestrated this whole thing. How humiliating. I have no idea why he'd agree to go along with it.

"I'm sorry. They shouldn't have done that." I stand and pick up the basketball. His face is apologetic, the muscles in his neck tighten as he swallows. Full lips part and I wait in the excruciating silence to hear what he has to say. Like maybe tonight wasn't so awful, but he says nothing.

"Gabby! Z! Open up." Nathan pounds on the gym door, his smiling face is smashed up against the glass. At least one person is genuinely excited to hang out with me tonight.

Zeke looks conflicted, unmoving, while Nathan keeps yelling for us to let him in.

I hold up my basketball like it represents our time together and toss it toward him. He catches it easily with one big hand, still holding his in the other. "Thank you for being so nice about the whole thing, but I don't need a pity date."

four

Gabby

"Morning," Blair calls out as she appears in the kitchen, Wes on her heels.

I straighten on the bar stool and take another drink from the mug in my hands. "Morning. You two look adorable." I smirk and Blair pulls on the hem of the long Valley basketball t-shirt. It looks like she literally took it off his back because her boyfriend wears only a pair of basketball shorts and a very satisfied smile.

He moves to the coffee machine and Blair takes the bar stool next to me. She slouches in her seat. "Last night was crazy. I've never seen so many people in one place in my life."

"It was a lot," I admit. "You want to head over to the gym and then grab brunch? I think a good run might clear the foam and alcohol from my head. I have to work tonight, too. Ugh."

"Can't. I have loads of laundry and packing to do. Actually, I wanted to talk to you about that."

"About offering to do my laundry?" I tease.

"No, although, if that green skirt you wore last week is dirty, I'm willing to wash it so I can wear it this week."

"You're in luck, I did laundry yesterday. Where are you and my fabulous green skirt going?" Blair and I have been swapping clothes since elementary school. Two closets are better than one.

"Did you ask her?" Katrina enters the kitchen with Joel just a step behind.

"Ask me what?" It suddenly feels like an ambush or maybe I'm just touchy from last night. I look from person to person trying to figure out what's going on.

Joel answers for the lot of them. "Spring break in Mexico. You in?"

Blair bounces beside me. "Is there any way you can get off work? Joel's family has a place and we're gonna go lie on the beach and drink piña coladas," she says dreamily.

"I don't know." The excitement in the room is contagious, not that I'd need any help getting excited about the idea of spring break in Mexico. Of course, I want nothing more than to go somewhere amazing with my friends for spring break. I mean, hell yeah, but I just started working at The Hideout and I have a sinking feeling the reason I'm on the schedule almost every day next week is because everyone else already put in to be off. "I work today, so I can ask. When are you leaving?"

"Tonight. Puh-leeeze." Blair's voice is pleading.

"You're *all* going?"

Blair nods and squeezes my hand. "It'll be so much fun."

"It sounds amazing, but I can't lose this job. My parents are holding firm on the whole not paying my rent thing. Let me send Brady a text and see if anyone can cover my shifts."

I'm not hopeful as I type out the message to my boss and press send. It's a darn shame too. I pick up my phone and add spring break to the list I'd started earlier this morning.

Nathan and Z enter the kitchen and we're just one big happy family all squeezed into the space. Zeke and I make eye contact for the briefest of moments before his gaze darts away. Eventually he rejoined the party last night, but we didn't speak again after I found out he'd been forced to act as my date. Instead, Nathan and I drank and danced until we were the last two people in the back yard.

"What is this?" Blair asks, looking down at my phone. "Do a keg stand, make out on campus—"

"Don't read them out loud," I plead. I'd written the list with a fresh determination to do everything I dreamt about before moving to Valley, holding nothing back, but this list is a little more detailed than I feel comfortable sharing over coffee with my best friends and their boyfriends.

"Seriously, what are these?" Blair bites her lip to try and hide her smile.

"Things I want to do before August."

"Why August?" Wes asks, holding the mug to his lips.

A glance around the room confirms everyone is

watching and listening intently. Except Zeke. "I want to start my senior year as a normal college kid. Not some sheltered weirdo."

A weirdo whose friends have to force guys to go on dates with her. A fresh wave of mortification rolls through me.

"And doing the walk of shame," Blair reads another item on the list. "Is going to make you normal?"

"The walk of awesome," Joel interjects.

"Exactly. See, how will I know if I think it's awesome or not unless I try it?"

"For all that is holy, don't take Joel's advice on anything. Especially that." That remark earns Wes the finger from Joel, but I don't cross it off my list.

"I bet we can accomplish almost every one of these," Katrina says as she looks over my shoulder. "On the beach in Mexico."

"Online dating?" Nathan crowds behind me and asks. "You're too hot for online dating. That's for chicks that use Snapchat filters and haven't updated their profile pic since they gained the freshman fifteen."

Katrina turns her nose up. "He's mostly right. I tried it a couple times and never once did I show up and think 'wow, he's even hotter in person.' I think it might be better for the post-college demographic."

"The point isn't that every item on the list will be amazing, just to do them so I can express an opinion. I don't want to be sitting around at parties while everyone talks about the crazy things they've done and all I can offer is the time I binge-watched all six seasons of *Jersey Shore* in one weekend."

"Cabs are here!" Nathan calls out with a fist pump as

bad as his fake Jersey accent.

The tension in my shoulders lifts as the room erupts with laughter and the guys take turns fist pumping. My phone vibrates on the counter and Blair and I read it together, our laughter dying at the same time.

"Sorry," she says and pushes her bottom lip out.

I let out a breath as I close out the message from my boss confirming there's no one to cover a spontaneous trip to Mexico. "It's fine. Maybe I'll tackle online dating first. It'll probably take me the entire time you're gone to set up my profile."

"Oooh, let's do that now." Blair claps her hands, eyes glittering with excitement.

"Yeah!" echoes Katrina.

Soon I'm flanked on either side by Blair and Katrine while the guys dig for food in the pantry and refrigerator.

"What's your type?" Katrina asks as Blair takes over my phone and downloads the dating app.

"I'm not really sure."

"Hmm. Let's start with basics. What does he look like?"

"I don't really care." I shrug.

Blair rolls her eyes. "Let me think, who's the last guy you dated?" A crease forms between her eyes. "Have you dated anyone since JT?"

I shake my head. Four very long, very single years.

"Who's JT?" Katrina asks.

"Gabby's high school boyfriend." She looks back to me. "Is that still your type?"

"I don't have a type." Which is mostly true. I haven't dated enough to compare my preferences.

"Okay then describe your perfect guy."

"I'm looking for fun and casual, not Mister Perfect."

Blair gives me her most determined glare. She's not letting me out of this, so I think for a moment, picturing all the reality TV and book boyfriends I've collected over the past few years. "Tall and muscular, for sure. I'm curvy and I don't want to feel like I'm going to crush some poor guy if I straddle him while doing the reverse cowgirl."

A choking noise across the kitchen makes us look up and Wes is wiping coffee off his chest. Oops, that was an overshare, but it's still true.

Katrina keeps going. "What about hair?"

"I don't really care."

She points to the guys. "Buzzed, short, medium, long. Take your pick. We've got prime examples of varying lengths here."

I look them over carefully, each one standing a little taller under my scrutiny. Nathan's long hair totally suits him, but I shake him off first. "Not long."

"What?" He scoffs and tucks a blonde strand behind his ears.

"I like short," I say reluctantly. "And I like the designs in Zeke's."

It's almost painful to offer him a compliment right now, but I really do like it. Zeke's hair is buzzed close to his head, but along the sides has a faint design. Each time I've seen him, the design has been different and always hardly noticeable, but it's there, the smallest hint that the man cares about his looks.

He stills at his name, protein drink in hand, and if it were possible to detect a blush on his black skin, I'm certain I could. I feel oddly proud that I've made him uncomfortable.

"Iiiiinteresting," Blair says, drawing out the word as she taps the screen. "Hobbies?"

"Art, reality TV, dancing… but those things don't matter. I'm not looking for anything serious, just someone to have fun with."

"I got this," Katrina says, taking my phone from Blair with a wicked smile.

She's quiet as she taps away furiously, her bottom lip pulled behind her teeth. "Okay. There."

She hands me the phone and Blair and I huddle together to read.

"Oh my God, Katrina."

"I know, right? I channeled my inner Vanessa."

"Pole dancing?" I ask.

Blair giggles beside me. "You described her as fun, adventurous, and spontaneous."

I groan.

"In the bedroom," Joel adds, and three heads pop up to look at him. "What? It's like fortune cookies, you always add 'in the bedroom' to the end of the adjectives chicks use to describe themselves."

"Done," Blair says, and I glance over to see my new profile published. Guess there's no backing out. "Now, let's focus on me."

Wes comes up behind Blair and wraps his arms around her. "No way, babydoll. No online dating for you."

She rolls her eyes at. "Simmer down. I just need to raid Gabby's closet before we leave. She has the best wardrobe."

The Tip-Off

That's me. Fun, adventurous, and spontaneous… in the closet.

"Your mom went all out." Blair picks through my closet, tossing items on the bed into two piles in front of where I lie, curled up, hugging a pillow and wishing I had time for a nap before work. Another dress is added to the stack at my feet. "This one is a maybe. I don't know if I have the curves to pull it off like you can," she says of the white cutout dress.

"She was so excited that I wanted to go shopping for school clothes that she booked an overnight trip in LA to do it."

"Fancy," Blair says. "How is Momma Brech, anyway?" Another dress and skirt make their way into the maybe pile. "Has she stopped tracking your location when you don't answer her calls?"

She isn't quite that bad, but Blair isn't far off. Nearly losing their only child made my parents a tad overprotective. Okay, not a tad. A lot overprotective. I get it, but it's suffocating. I think my moving out will be good for all of us. "She's good. Dad finally convinced her to take a new job that gets her out of the house, so she's a little less focused on monitoring my every move."

"With a closet like this, I can't say that I blame her. College Gabby dresses like a hoochie momma," she teases with a wink.

"Says the girl raiding my hoochie momma closet." I stand and grab a bag off the floor and then hold it out by the handles in her direction. "Here. Try these."

Her eyes light up, but she bites her lip. "I can't wear something you haven't even taken the tags off."

"What's the difference? I haven't worn most of the items in my closet yet." I shake the bag and she finally takes a step forward. With a look inside the bag, she squeals, putting a sound to the excitement on her face. My best friend is easily excitable, but the slinky blue dress she's holding is pretty damn squeal-worthy.

She holds it up in front of her and stares at her reflection in the mirror.

"That one is gonna look great on you. Just don't let Wes rip it off you. I want to wear it once I get a nice summer tan."

Still clutching the dress in one hand, Blair sits on the bed and hugs me tightly with her free arm. "I'm so glad you're here at Valley. I really wish you were coming to Mexico, though. I feel bad leaving you all alone."

"Oh please, I'll be fine. Work, sleep, catch up on Netflix."

Blair looks unconvinced.

"Don't worry about me. Go have fun and promise to drunk dial me at least once."

"Deal." She smooths a hand over my comforter, tracing the beaded flower design. "You know who else will be here this week?"

"Who?"

"Zeke!" she says with far too much excitement.

"Yeah, speaking of, could you guys have not found someone else to be my date last night?"

Blair frowns. "I thought you liked Zeke."

"He's okay," I lie easily. "But he's not into me like that and last night was humiliating the way you guys forced him to be my date. God, I'm the most pathetic college junior ever."

"Stop it. You are not. And no one made Zeke be your date. He's a good guy, but I've never known him to do anything just because someone told him to. I think he likes you."

Sweet Blair, always the optimist and ever since she met Wes, a hopeless romantic. "I think you've fallen down the love tunnel." I smack her lightly on the forehead.

Blair squeezes my hand and gives me a reassuring smile. "Are you okay?"

I hate that she can read me so well. I don't want to be upset at Zeke's rejection, but I just can't help it. There were moments last night that I thought we clicked. On the plus side, it won't be hard to avoid seeing him while everyone is gone. It isn't like he's going to come looking for me.

"I'm fine. Just cranky. I'm going to shower." I squeeze her tightly. I have no idea what I'm going to do without her this week. She's my lifeline. My person. "I love you. Be careful down there."

"Yes, Mom." She rolls her eyes. We separate and she goes back to inspecting the piles of clothes on the bed as I duck into the bathroom.

five

Zeke

I'm getting back from a late workout when the guys are loading up for their trip. "Sure you won't come with us?" Wes asks. "One last spring break vacation together."

"Nah, I've got a full week of an empty house, empty weight room, and empty court – that's my dream vacation."

Nathan steps next to me and shoves his hands in his short pockets. "Not entirely empty, bro."

"You're staying?"

Wes chuckles, making me realize I did shit to hide the disappointment in my tone. It's not that I don't like Nathan, I was just excited for a week of no distractions.

"I don't have the cash to blow."

I know full well Joel wouldn't let him pay for

anything if he went, but I get not wanting to be a charity case.

"He's just sticking around to hang with Gabby," Wes adds, earning a smack on the arm from his girlfriend.

Nathan's smile is on the embarrassed side, but he doesn't deny it, just shakes his head and heads toward the house.

"I think it's sweet he doesn't want her to be here by herself," Blair says after he's gone. "She's still adjusting, and I don't think she likes being alone."

Maybe it's my own guilt for the way last night went down, but Blair's gaze seems to bore into me as she provides the last bit of information on her best friend.

"Let's load up," Joel calls out. He's wearing Ray-Bans and a vacation smile.

Blair hangs back as the rest of the group gets in the car.

"Have a good trip." I take a step toward the house and she calls out, "Zeke, hold up."

I like Blair, I do, but the look on her face tells me she's about to ask me a favor I'm not going to like.

"I have a favor."

Called that. I blow out a breath before I ask, "What's up?"

"Can you check in on Gabby this week? I know you're busy preparing for the draft, but I'd feel better about leaving her if I knew she had someone looking out for her."

I jab a thumb back to the house. "Nathan doesn't have shit going on this week. Why not ask him?"

"Because…" She worries her lip before continuing. "I trust you and I know you'll keep her safe."

I run a hand over my head and sigh. Nathan can barely look after himself so yeah, I get it. And it isn't that I mind doing it, but I'm probably the last person she wants checking in on her. I slept like shit last night, Gabby's ocean blue eyes filled with so much hurt and anger as she fled from the gym haunted me all damn night.

I stare past Blair's head to Wes sitting in the car. He watches our interaction carefully through the backseat window. I'd do anything for Wes, we've had each other's backs for four years. No questions asked, whatever the other needed. And he'd do anything for Blair. "Yeah, okay. I'll check on her while you're gone."

Blair lets out a high-pitched squeal and throws her arms around my neck. "Thank you so much. You're the best."

She runs off toward the car and hops in, giving me a little wave and a big grin as they pull away from the curb.

And just like that, my week of focusing on myself is shot to shit.

Three days later I'm sitting at The Hideout doing my first check-in on Gabby and also meeting with my agent. Two birds, one stone and all that.

"My assistant Colleen tells me you still haven't set up a social media account." Sara's expression is amused, but her tone is serious. "If you don't want to do it yourself, we can hire someone to do it, but having a social media presence is non-negotiable. Most college athletes already have them and boast big followings. It's good for endorsements. Colleen emailed you some photos with suggestions for posts, but mix in a little of your personality, too. You have the week off. Hang with your friends, snap a couple pictures and post them. People want to know what it's like to be you."

Sara Icoa, my agent, is no-nonsense. I love that about her. Unless she's telling me things I don't want to hear.

I grumble as I take another large bite from my salad. Social media is just one more thing pulling my attention from practicing, and I've already received plenty of endorsement offers, but I don't argue against her logic. I'm paying her for a reason.

She offers me an apologetic 'this is just how it is' look before moving on to the next topic. "I anticipate you'll get your official invitation to the NBA Combine later this month, so keep up with your workouts and the diet."

I swallow the soggy vegetables in my mouth and prepare to speak, but Sara holds up a hand. "I know, I know, I don't need to remind you, but I feel better having said it."

She closes the portfolio in front of her and I'm struck with how young she looks in her jeans and white t-shirt, hair pulled back in a tight ponytail. It's only her third year as an agent, but she's been just as good and thorough as she promised. "This is gonna be fun."

"It'll be fun on June twentieth." The date of the draft. Until then, it's a singular focus. I'm so close, no holding back now.

"Can I get you anything else?" Gabby's bubbly voice

asks, standing at the foot of our booth, eyes never leaving Sara.

Sara politely declines and hands Gabby the empty salad plate in front of her and then looks to me. I could go for dessert or maybe a cheeseburger, hell, I'd even eat another salad, but I just shake my head.

Gabby drops the check. "No rush. You two are the only thing stopping Brady from sending me home early."

I glance around The Hideout. Place looks weird so dead, but most students left in search of fun or family over spring break.

When I turn back, Sara has her wallet out, paying our check.

"I've got the tip," I offer and drop some cash on the table.

Brady, the manager of The Hideout, approaches our table with a wide smile. "Zeke. Good to see you. How've you been? We haven't seen you in a while."

"Doing good, Mr. Williams, just been busy."

"Ah, I bet. Number one draft pick right here in my restaurant. It's exciting." His eyes crinkle as his lips pull into a wide smile.

I glance at Sara who's holding in a laugh.

"It is. Thank you."

"Was everything okay? Did Gabby take good care of you?"

I glance behind him at the wait station where Gabby briefly meets my gaze and then rolls her eyes.

"Yes, sir."

"Alright." He knocks on the table. "If you need anything, you let me know."

I shake my head as he retreats.

"Better get used to the attention," Sara says and then pulls out her phone. "Alright, let's talk schedule." She gives me the rundown for the next few weeks.

Adrenaline courses through my veins as she gives me dates for interviews with teams that are likely to be picking in the top five. It's finally here, only weeks away, and I'm so ready.

"Alright, I'm sorry to eat and run, but I've gotta drive to Phoenix for another meeting. Let me know if you need anything." She scoots out of the booth and I follow suit. "Don't forget what I said about social media. If you haven't created an account by tomorrow, I'll assume you want me to hire someone to do it for you."

"Thank you for driving down," I say. "Have a safe trip back."

I sit back down in the booth, pop a cucumber into my mouth, and withdraw my phone from my pocket. As promised, Colleen sent over a dozen images and post suggestions. At the very bottom in all caps, she's written: *P.S. DON'T FORGET TO ADD AT LEAST FIVE HASHTAGS TO EACH POST. P.S.S. HAVE FUN!*

Fuck my life. Looks like my days of avoiding social media are officially over.

Six

Gabby

"Hey," I say tentatively as I stand at the edge of Zeke's table. He's been sitting here by himself staring at his phone for over twenty minutes.

He looks up and the scowl on his face falls away. "Hey, Gabby."

"Did your phone do something to hurt your feelings or is that just your standard glare?"

Setting it down on the table, Zeke lets out a rush of air before answering. "I don't understand Instagram and hashtags - people are still using those? I thought it died off when people started using it in everyday speech." He makes the symbol with his hands. "Hashtag, I don't get it."

I resist the urge to laugh. Barely. He looks so defeated. The best college basketball player in the whole country is frustrated over an app I mastered at thirteen. It's a nice boost to my fragile ego.

"I'm closing out, so Savannah is going to take over your table." I take a step away only to find my boss, Brady, scrutinizing my every move. Everyone knows Zeke is his favorite customer, he makes no effort to hide his giant man crush. Brady cranes his neck to get a better view of the situation and I let out a sigh and turn around.

"Would you like some help?"

My offer seems to take him by surprise, and he looks me over slowly. His gaze holds a second longer before his eyes flit away. "It's alright. I'll ask one of the guys later."

Maybe it's the fact he wants me to leave, or the fact my boss will appreciate me more if he sees me buddying up to Zeke, I can't say for sure, but instead of leaving him alone, I take a seat across from him, pick up his phone and hold it out. "Hashtag procrastination."

"I don't even have any followers yet, so it's fine. It can wait."

I pull my phone from my apron pocket. "What's your username?"

"Just my name, all one word," he answers.

"There." I set my phone down after following his new account. "Now, your fans demand more."

He smiles a bit as he takes his phone and opens the app. I feel my phone vibrate next to me and know he's followed me back. Is it pathetic to be excited that I'm the first person the great Zeke Sweets followed on Instagram? Maybe I'll get a byline in his Wikipedia page someday.

"Do you have a photo picked out for your profile and

first post?"

"I have some options."

It takes five painful minutes where I want to take his phone and do it for him, before Zeke has uploaded a profile picture, copied the text his agent suggested for his bio, and selected a photo for his first post.

"Let me," I demand when he's hovering over the keys trying to figure out what to write below the posed photo of him in his Valley jersey. It's a promo shot I've seen before. Zeke looks big and intimidating, muscular arms crossed over his broad chest, and mouth pulled into a determined line.

He hands over the phone without protest, but he eagle-eyes my every tap.

"See you at tip-off. #ballislife, #focused, #thetip-off, #valleyu, #firstpost."

"Wow," he finally says when I'm done. He takes his phone and stares at the still un-published post. "You came up with all of that in like five seconds?"

"Not my first time, big guy."

I hear the sound the app makes when he publishes the post and he actually lets out a sigh like it's been an exhausting effort.

"So that was your agent?"

"Yeah."

"That's cool. I expected her to be in a suit and to scream out things like 'Show Me the Money!' Does she have a mission statement?"

He chuckles. "Jerry Maguire."

"Ooh right. Blair mentioned how much you like Tom Cruise. So, what kinds of things does a sports agent do for you? Isn't the draft still a few months away?"

"Gets me practices with teams, interviews, social media shit."

"So, it's not just an Instagram-specific hatred?" I ask, amused.

"I've never used any of them before today. Don't see the point."

"You're kidding, right?"

He lifts a shoulder and lets it drop.

"Social media is huge and growing every day. The big NBA guys have followings the size of some countries! I read somewhere the market value for a single Lebron James tweet is over one hundred and twenty-five thousand dollars."

"I know, I got practically the same spiel from Sara. I just wanna play ball, not post cheesy photos of myself."

"The NBA is a business, like anything else. Think of Instagram as an extension of the interviews. Plus, it's a cool way to promote yourself and let people know a little about you. A behind the scenes look, if you will."

He holds his phone out toward me so I can see the screen and the notifications of new followers and likes.

"My work here is done." I stand, pocket my phone, and the check holder with the signed receipt for their meal. "Next time, I'll show you the apps you can download to automatically curate the best hashtags."

"Now you tell me," he mumbles to my back. I'm a few steps away when he says my name. His low voice caresses each syllable. I take a deep breath before I turn to face him. His eyes are sincere and apologetic. "Thank you for this, and I'm really sorry about the other night. I had fun shooting hoops with you."

"Yeah, me too."

seven

Gabby

$\mathcal{S}$ince I moved to Valley before the end of the semester, I'm currently living alone. The plan is for Blair and Vanessa to move in over the summer, but in the meantime, my apartment is pretty bare and lonely.

And, I hate to say it, but living alone isn't as much fun as I thought it'd be. From the safety of my parents' house, it seemed so grown up and awesome. Bills, coming home when and if I wanted, leaving messes with no one to bug me about dirty dishes in the sink or laundry sitting in a clothes basket were just a few bullet items that somehow represented a life I'd been missing out on.

Turns out, what I'd been missing out on is a lot of sleepless nights. Every noise, and there are plenty living in an apartment, makes me jump, but even worse is the eerie quiet. Too much time alone with my own thoughts and insecurities leads to a lot of late-night TV watching to drown out the silence. I'm going to be a walking zombie before Blair and Vanessa move in at the end of the semester.

I stifle a yawn as I walk around the back of The White House and enter the back yard.

"You came!" Nathan calls as he exits the house carrying two beers. Bright blue swim trunks hang from his hips and I gawk, mouth open, as he walks toward me. "Here ya go."

I drop my bag and towel by the large, sparkling pool, take the beer even though it's barely ten o'clock in the morning, and shake my head before popping the top. "Nathan, your abs have abs."

He winks. "Abs for Gabs."

Just when I'm about to call him out on his ego, he looks down, a shy smile tugs at his lips.

"Gabby, you know Tanner Shaw and Marcus Malone?" He motions to the pool where the guys are hanging out.

Shaw raises his beer and Malone waves in greeting.

"Hey!" A trio of voices draws my attention to the slider Nathan just came out of. The three girls are bikini-clad, hair pulled up in messy buns, and one of them carries a large unicorn floatie.

"Shelly, Tara, Simone, you girls know Gabby? She's a friend of Blair's from high school."

We offer awkward hellos and I take a seat next to the pool, dipping my feet in the cool water. Before I've finished my first beer, more girls have shown up and everyone has moved to the pool for water ball, which is basically just basketball in five feet of water. Two floating baskets are positioned at each end of the large pool and the teams are divided up evenly. Shaw and Nathan are on one team with Shelly and Simone against everyone else. I'm sitting on the edge cheering them on and occasionally making a final decision on fouls.

Nathan splashes me playfully as he swims back on defense. "You want in this game? Malone needs all the help he can get."

"Next game," I say and stand. "I'm gonna go get another beer."

As I enter the house, the blast of air conditioning on my wet legs pulls a shiver from me. I toss my empty in the recycling and grab another beer from the fridge, but instead of heading back out, I walk toward the noise coming from the TV room.

Zeke's reclined in a large leather chair, phone in hand, a deep line of annoyance creased between his eyes.

"Hey," I say, hovering in the doorway. "Hashtag blues?"

He nods without looking up. "Sara wasn't all that impressed with the numbers for my first post, she wants me to post something more personal." He turns the phone so I can see his screen. It's a picture of Joel kicked back on a lounger, perfect body on display, the beach and ocean as a backdrop. "Is this the shit people really want to see?"

I walk all the way into the room and take the seat next to him. As I place my beer in the armrest cupholder, I feel his eyes on me. I realize that my low-cut swimsuit is doing nothing to conceal my nipples' reaction to the cool air at the same time he does, which only makes them tighten harder. His gaze holds a beat longer before he looks away.

"Maybe I should just pay someone to do it for me." His low voice rakes over my skin.

"I have an idea." At my words, he looks to me hopefully, and I stand. "Come on."

It takes some convincing to get Zeke in swim trunks. Though, Lord knows why because he is *wearing* the things.

"Z!" the guys call out to him when they catch sight of us coming outside. For a guy that seems to prefer to be alone, he's got a lot of people just dying to hang with him.

The game is put on pause as Zeke and I get into the water and are added to teams. Nathan swims up to me and whispers, "You're some sort of miracle worker getting Zeke to join. He never gets in the water."

"Really?"

He nods just as the game starts back up. It doesn't take long before Zeke forgets that he's a grumpy fun-hater and starts to get into it.

Nathan and Zeke communicate wordlessly, passing the mini basketball around and moving in the water with ease. The other guys are good, too, but Nathan and Zeke have the kind of comfort and compatibility that speaks to their years of being teammates. It's damn impressive and I give up any pretenses of playing. I'm not providing a lot of value, anyway, occasionally stealing a bad pass and then quickly sending the ball sailing to someone else, so I slip out and grab my phone from a lounge chair.

Every time Zeke gets possession, I snap as many

pictures as I can, hoping at least one comes out capturing him as a fun, carefree college guy. I gotta admit, being his personal photographer isn't a bad gig. And when he's smiling and having fun, I find myself wanting to be around him even more. So does everyone else. They slap his back, give him fist bumps, the girls get handsy on defense and bat their eyelashes. How can a guy that's so insistent on keeping people at arm's length be so well liked?

When the game is over, Zeke pulls himself from the pool. His wet body glistens as the water drips off him. He shakes his head in my direction with a smile on his face.

"Have fun?" I sing-song.

"I did," he says and nods slowly like he's equally as surprised.

"Well, I got some great options." I hold up my phone and then motion for him to take a seat on a lounge chair.

Zeke swipes through the photos a dozen times, his face pure concentration.

"Do you want me to pick?" I offer.

"Yeah, I don't know what I'm looking for." He stops on a picture and hands me the phone. "I like this one. That dunk was awesome. I can't believe you captured it."

"That one is good, but the focus needs to be you. I can't see your face in this one." I go to my favorite and show him. "I like this one."

"I don't even have the ball."

I roll my eyes. "No, but you're smiling and having fun."

He grumbles.

"How about we post them both?" I offer as a compromise.

"Yeah, alright."

I text both pictures to his phone and show him how to add more than one photo to a post and then we download a hashtag app, so he doesn't have to try and come up with the clever tags on his own.

"Thank you," he says quietly when we're finished. I can feel his eyes on mine, and I take a deep breath before I allow myself to meet them.

"You're welcome."

I can feel Zeke's desire to run off even before he announces he's gonna shower. The crowd outside has doubled since the game ended and people are standing around, drinks in hand.

I watch Zeke disappear into the house and lean back on the lounge chair taking in the easy way everyone interacts. Every person I've met today has been friendly and welcoming, but I'm still not part of their circle. Not really. When I'm introduced the byline is always, *Blair's friend*, Gabby.

Nathan catches my eye from across the patio and motions me over.

"Gabby, baby, wanna be on my team for beer pong?" He shakes a plastic cup at me.

"You know it." I grab the cup and take one last fleeting look toward the door where Zeke disappeared.

eight

Zeke

Lying on my back, I toss the basketball into the air and catch it. The sound of leather gliding over my calloused palms and off my fingers doesn't do shit to block out the noise from the party outside. For all the fancy shit in this house – double insulated walls didn't make the cut.

I grab my headphones and phone from my desk and settle back on the bed. When the music filters through, I close my eyes. I've always loved music, but it's become so much more in these past years. Shut the world out, music on. Just me and the melodies. The soundtrack of my life is a mixtape of other people's experiences. A little screwed up? Maybe, but I've got too much on the line to get swept up in the noise.

The music isn't working as quickly tonight. When

sleep doesn't come, I take them off and note that the racket outside has stopped. The wall vibrates with the shut of Nathan's door. Party's over. The guy might keep me awake with his late nights, but it's a comfort to know he's here and safe.

Nathan and I are the least close of the guys in the house. I've got a single focus and he does too, they're just not the same focus. And his, though not my problem anymore, still annoys me. He's so talented and he just doesn't seem to care. Sure, he works hard in practice and he is a huge asset in games, but all the rest of the time? It's a fifty-fifty chance he's either getting wasted or working on his ab game.

Some days I roll downstairs at five a.m. and he's already up working out like he gives a shit, and other days he's passed out on the couch, beer still in hand, and reeking of smoke. I don't understand why someone with so much talent would waste it with a half-assed mentality.

My phone vibrates from another notification and I press ignore like I did all the other times. How Gabby was able to orchestrate a mini photo shoot, make a post, and suddenly the whole damn world knows I'm on Instagram, is beyond me.

I stopped keeping track when it went over the ten thousand mark. Even Joel, who should be lying on a beach somewhere drinking Mai Tais or some expensive, fruity drink, found me. Doesn't make any sense to me that people want to see more of my personal life.

Sara is excited though. She's already demanded more casual pictures showing my life as a "typical college athlete." There is nothing typical about my life.

Movement next door catches my attention and I listen intently while I try and figure out if it's Nathan settling in for the night or if I need to check on him. But the noise is coming from the other side of the wall. Standing, I walk to my bedroom door and open it a crack. There's definitely someone in there. Shit, did Nathan pass out in the wrong room? Wouldn't be the first time.

I head to Wes' room, push open the door and let out a sigh before saying, "Yo, Nate, you're in the wrong—"

But the end of that sentence gets lost somewhere between Gabby's bare legs and the curves that are on full display in the white one-piece swimsuit she's wearing. She's bent over, head peering in an oversized bag on the bed.

"Just me," she squeaks. "I texted Blair to make sure it was okay. Wes said it was cool if I just crashed here. I didn't want to worry about finding a sober ride."

I nod. "Sorry, yeah, of course."

"Wait!" she calls as I'm backtracking out of the room like there's a fire. When I turn around, she stands up straight. "Do you have headphones I can borrow?" She bites her lip because it's not really a question of if I have headphones, she already knows the answer, but she rambles on pleading her case anyway. "I can't sleep without music and I left mine at home."

"Sure."

I lead the way to my room. The lights are off, so I turn on a lamp and open the desk drawer, presenting her with the options.

She laughs. "Why do you always wear the same ones when you have so many?"

The Tip-Off

I shrug, eyeing my red Beats. "They're my favorites."

Gabby rifles through my headphones before pulling out a pair of earbuds and holding them up as if asking for approval.

"You can keep those," I tell her. "The cord always gets tangled and takes forever to get straight."

"That's not necessary. I have some at home but thank you for letting me borrow them."

With a smile, she heads toward the door and my chest tightens.

"Want some new music?" I ask, surprising even myself by the offer.

She studies me carefully, eyebrows pulling together in confusion, before responding, "Sure. Whatcha got?"

I sit on the bed and Gabby does the same, watching me as I pull out my phone and scroll through my many playlists. "What are you in the mood for?"

She shrugs. "I like everything. Surprise me."

"Try this." I hold my phone out for her to see.

Instead of taking my phone, or pulling up the app and finding my playlist, she scoots farther onto the bed and plugs the headphones into my phone, puts one earbud in, and offers me the other.

My large frame takes up most of the mattress all by itself so even though Gabby is pint-sized, I'm basically on top of her as I settle back and take the earbud. Our bodies touch from hip to shoulder. Her soft curves mold against me and I fumble with the earbud.

As I pick it up, the cord tangles and I let out an exasperated groan as I tug on it as if to say, "See, I told you." My effort to get it untangled is half-assed though because Gabby hits play, and the sound of Billie Eilish relaxes me and Gabby too from the looks of it. Her body melts into the bed and she lies back, giving me little choice but to do the same. I scoot up against the headboard, still mostly upright so it isn't like we're lying together exactly. Because that would be weird, right?

"I didn't picture you for a Billie Eilish fan."

"I like everything. Well, except country."

She smiles and then her eyes flutter closed, dark lashes against ivory skin. Her face is bare, free of the heavy makeup she usually uses to cover the scars. I can't see them from this side, something I'm sure she considered when she sat on the bed. Gabby is always thinking of her scars. The way she stands in a room, the way she holds her head when talking to people, the nervous habit she has of playing with her hair and holding it over that side of her face. Yeah, I've noticed. I'd blame it on my observant nature, but I'm not sure that's entirely all there is to it.

The song ends and I expect her to open her eyes, take the headphones and her hot ass back to the other side of the wall. She doesn't and the next track starts. Am I an ass if I nudge her and tell her I'm ready to go to sleep? Technically I don't have to be anywhere at a specific time tomorrow, but I like the schedule of a workout first thing in the morning, so I've got my alarm set for the usual five a.m. wakeup.

We've listened to four more songs before I've summoned the courage to politely inform her that I need to get to sleep. At my touch on her upper arm, her eyes fly open and meet mine. The words I'd planned are stuck in my throat.

She sits up suddenly. "What was that?"

The Tip-Off

Nathan's voice filters through the wall – a cross between a cry and a yell.

"Shit." I'm on my feet and rushing to his room. I reach him just before he rips the covers from his bed. I know the routine and his next step is flipping the mattress. He swings, arms wild, looking to connect with anything. He clips the side of my face before I get both arms pinned. "Nate, you're good, man. You're good."

His eyes are glossy, and he smells like smoke and rubbing alcohol. He goes limp and settles back on the bed.

"I'm fine." His words are terse as he grabs the blanket and pulls it up over him. "I'm *fine*," he says again when I haven't moved. "Go away."

Gabby's in the hall watching with wide eyes when I close his door. Fuck, if she'd gone in there and he'd clipped her instead of me… I don't want to think about it.

"Is he okay?" she asks, her voice small and wavering.

I walk into my room, her right behind me before I answer. "He'll be alright."

"Does that happen a lot?"

I shrug, trying to play it off. Nathan and I aren't close, but I'm not going to tell his shit. "He'll sleep it off and be good in the morning."

She's staring at me, a list of questions she doesn't ask marring her features. "You're bleeding."

My hand goes to my mouth where he caught me, and my fingers bring back blood. "He just grazed me. I'm gonna get this cleaned up." I nod to the headphones. "They're all yours."

nine

Gabby

"Hey, you stay over last night?" Nathan asks as he enters the kitchen. His long hair is damp, and he pulls a grey t-shirt over his head.

"Yeah, it was late, and I didn't want to call an Uber, so I called Blair and Wes said I could crash in his room."

I wonder if he remembers last night, if he knows I was just outside his door when Zeke was restraining him, but there's no indication from his expression that he feels embarrassed and I think he would be if he thought I'd heard.

He settles next to me after getting a Gatorade from the refrigerator. "Whatcha got going on today?"

"I work tonight." I shrug. "Nothing until then."

"Cool. You can hang with me this afternoon."

I follow him out to the pool where he tosses the shirt

he'd just pulled on less than two minutes ago. "Coming in?"

"My suit's upstairs."

"So, go put it on or just wear your bra and underwear. Honestly, it's the same thing."

"Not the same at all. Cotton panties do not look flattering when they're wet."

He smirks. "I beg to differ."

I push at his shoulder and he jumps into the pool and disappears underwater for a few long moments. I take a seat on the edge and dip my feet in. It's already hot outside and the water feels great. When he resurfaces, it's with a glint in his blue eyes.

"Oh no. No, you don't Nathan Payne," I protest with a squeal as he uses my legs to pull me into the pool fully dressed.

My jean shorts and t-shirt cling to my body. "You punk. Now the only clothes I brought are wet."

"Should have taken them off."

I pull myself, ungracefully, to sit next to the pool and wring out my shirt the best I can. Nathan hops out too, grabs his cigarettes, and sits beside me. He lights up and takes a long puff before exhaling. The smoke filters out into a cloud above us.

"How can you be this amazing athlete with a body to kill and still smoke like a chimney?"

Once again, I'm reminded of last night and how panicked he'd looked. I wish he'd confide in me, but sometimes being a good friend is just being there.

He takes a long drag, cheeks hollow before he lets it out with a mocking smile. "Everyone's got vices. This is mine. What's yours?"

"Reality TV and shopping."

His lips curve up. "Kardashians and couture?"

"I'm not even going to question how you know the word couture." I hold my hand out. "Let me try."

He hesitates, stares at the cigarette between his fingers and then me before shaking his head and handing it over. "Don't inhale."

"Isn't that the point?" I ask before disregarding his advice and taking a long drag. When the smoke burns down my chest, I cough and sputter for several long minutes while Nathan laughs at me. When I can speak, I say, "Well, that's one item I can cross off the list for good."

We sit in a comfortable silence until I ask, "What do you have going on today?"

"Whole lot of nothing. Some of the guys who stayed in Valley this week were thinking of going to Prickly Pear tonight. You interested?"

"I've gotta work, remember?" I bump his shoulder with mine.

"We probably won't even go until eleven or so. You can meet us there."

I catch a ride from a coworker to the Prickly Pear. It's a hole in the wall bar that is more popular with the Valley townies than college students, or so I'm told.

"You sure you don't want to come in for a drink?" I ask Savannah. She's a great work friend, but so far, we haven't hung outside of The Hideout. She's dating a guy on the Valley hockey team and her nights off seem to revolve around whatever he has planned.

"Wish I could. I promised Smith I'd help him meal prep and watch game footage. He's obsessed with making the most of his offseason." She parks the car in front of the bar. "Are you sure they're here? The place looks pretty dead."

I glance down at my phone and then scan the parking lot. I texted Nathan an hour ago and still haven't heard back from him. "That must be them." I point to an SUV with a Valley basketball license plate. I take a breath and open the door. "Thanks for the ride."

Loud, country music greets me as I enter the bar. I hover in the entrance glancing around the place until I find the table of Valley basketball players, but no Nathan. I walk toward them with all the confidence I can muster. Tanner Shaw greets me with his easy smile. "Hey, Gabby."

"Hey, guys." I wave as everyone at the table stares at me. "Have you seen Nathan?"

The guy sitting next to Shaw speaks after chuckling softly. "Last I saw him he was passed out on the floor."

"At The White House?"

"Nah, baseball house."

Guess that explains why he hasn't texted. "Okay, thanks."

I take a step back feeling all sorts of awkward for coming here only to be stood up, but Shaw stands and says, "Have a seat. I'll get another chair."

I hold up my phone and motion to the door. "I'm just gonna check on Nathan."

He waves me off. "He's fine, just got started too early today. The guy was doing shots before lunch."

I find myself seated at the table and introductions are made. The group of freshman and sophomore basketball players are nice. One of them grabs another glass and fills it with beer from the pitcher on the table. I shoot off a quick text to check on Nathan. Shaw and the others are playing it off like it's totally fine, but shots at noon and passing out early? That doesn't sound fine.

Me: Did Nathan make it back to the house?

Zeke: No, I haven't seen him all day.

Me: Could you walk over to the baseball house and check on him? He was supposed to meet me at Prickly Pear, but the guys said he was passed out on the floor over there. I'm worried about him. Is that normal for him?

Five minutes later, Zeke sends a text to let me know he found Nathan and got him back to The White House, he ignores my last question.

Shaw pours me a second beer, which I drink more freely now that I know Nathan is okay. Nothing seems to be going according to plan lately but making the most of it seems to be the new theme of my life.

The Tip-Off

Zeke

Gabby: The young guys are more fun than you.

A second later, a picture comes through. Her and Shaw are holding their beers up high and cheesing for the camera.

Me: Everyone is more fun than me.

Gabby: You say that like you don't have a choice in the matter. Come hang out.

Me: With the rookies? No thanks.

Gabby: Fun hater. We could get another picture for your adoring Insta fans.

A few minutes later, another text comes in.

Gabby: Are you on your way know?

Gabby: Shit. Nowe

Gabby: Ugggggghhhh

Gabby: NOW

Me: You're not driving, right?

Gabby: Nope.

Me: How are you getting home?

Gabby: I'll catch a ride back with one of the guys.

She doesn't text again, and I lay back on my bed listening to music and tossing a ball into the air, wondering if she's gonna be okay with my rookie teammates. I can almost see Blair's pleading eyes to watch out for her friend.

I put the ball down, stand, and take the six steps necessary to get to Nathan's room. He's still passed out on the bed in the same position I put him in. I don't get it.

Partying with friends, letting loose, I get. But this? This doesn't look like fun; it looks like something else entirely.

"Back later, buddy," I say to the silence.

Prickly Pear is as dead as the rest of the town, though Gabby and the guys would be easy to spot even if it were packed. Somehow, she's got all four of them on their feet and dancing on the small makeshift dance floor. Dancing badly. Real badly. Gabby doesn't seem to mind, the girl is all smiles.

With a nod to the bartender, I take off in their direction. When Gabby sees me, her lips pull apart and her smile grows wider. She launches herself at me, throwing her arms around my neck and pressing our bodies together in the process. She's like a mini-tornado, but she feels like a welcome disturbance to my steady routine.

"You actually came!" she says when she pulls back.

"Look at you," Shaw says. "Want a beer?"

When I accept, Shaw and Datson lead me to their table and a glass is thrust in front of me and filled. I don't drink much, even in the offseason, so the guys are grinning like I'm about to do something really crazy by having one beer.

"I think Cannon is in love." I follow Datson's line of vision to the dance floor where Gabby and Cannon have spread out using the entire space for some big dance moves that are earning laughs and strange looks from everyone in the bar.

"I think he's not the only one," Shaw says. "I finally figured out what it takes to get you out of the house." Shaw raises his eyebrows and nods toward Gabby. "Not that I can blame you. She's the hottest girl here. Hottest girl at Valley, probably, at least from the right side."

I say nothing, though his remark about her scars pisses me off. I take another drink and do my best to keep my eyes anywhere but on Gabby. She's doing some sort of moonwalk spin move combo so not watching isn't an easy feat.

"You gonna deny it?" Shaw presses.

Damn, I wish I had my headphones so I could drown him out.

"Of course not. Gabby's beautiful. I'm not blind."

"Just celibate," Datson pipes in.

"Is it a voluntary celibacy or have you just been spending too much time around Wes and Joel?"

I glare at him, waiting for him to explain what the hell he means. My boys are both in relationships – legit ones that I don't see ending any time soon.

"Everyone knows you don't hang around guys with girlfriends. They seem hotter because they're unobtainable, therefore making you look like a chump."

I laugh against my better judgment and Shaw's twisted logic. Though, I can attest that being unobtainable sometimes makes girls a little more interested. Though, usually for all the wrong reasons.

My rule against dating in college has resulted in plenty of unwanted ball honeys trying to prove they were different, special, or just more persistent than the others. The thing with being unobtainable though is it'll only make a person work harder for so long. When they realize it's not a game or a front, they lose interest. Or, that's been my experience. After four years of turning down girls, there are currently zero trying to get in my pants. Not that it matters since I'd turn them away. I haven't been a total saint, but I've been smart enough to hook up with girls who have no idea or just don't care, who I am.

"Well, if you're going to just sit here, mind if I make a move?"

"She's out of your league, rookie."

I glare at him, but Shaw's a cocky motherfucker, so he just smiles as he fires back, "Yours too."

Don't I know it.

My attention goes back to Gabby. She's headed our direction, singing along to the music, dancing even as she walks. She stops momentarily and her eyes flutter closed as she loses herself to the beat. Hips sway, long blonde hair tosses from side to side with her ass. She's a goddamn sight and there's no way I'm letting these assholes near her. Blair would kill me.

The Tip-Off

"Damn." I don't look over to verify where he's looking, but since his words echo my thoughts, I assume Shaw's watching her too. He drains the beer in his hand and scoots his chair back. "Last chance before I move in."

I place a hand on his shoulder and stand. As I walk away, I hear Shaw's annoying voice, "Knew you had it in you."

ten

Gabby

"We're gonna head back to the baseball house."

Shaw approaches the bar where Z and I are sitting huddled together looking through the dozen or more pictures I took trying to show Zeke out having fun with his teammates. He said hell no when I suggested a photo op with the other guys. So instead the pictures are of Zeke by himself trying to act casual and comfortable when he's obviously anything but. No surprise that we're struggling to agree on a picture we both like.

"Thanks for letting me crash. I had fun."

"Any time." Shaw smiles and moves in for a drunken hug, wrapping his arms around me and squeezing. He's warm and I can feel his muscles working under the plain white t-shirt. Zeke clears his throat, but Shaw continues to hold me tight for a good three seconds more before he eases his hold on me and looks to Zeke. "Why don't you guys come back with us? It's a good night for beers on the patio."

"No." "Yes!" Zeke and I say at the same time.

His big pouty lips pull into an adorable frown that isn't the least bit intimidating. Well, to me. Shaw takes another step back as Z asks, "How are you getting there?"

"Oh, uh." I look to Shaw for help.

He stares down at his shoes sheepishly. "Can you give us a lift?"

Light brown eyes flit from Shaw to me and his big chest heaves with a sigh. I like him like this – out pretending to have fun, socializing, being coerced into being the sober driver.

"Shotgun," I call.

At the baseball house, Zeke parks and gets out of the car with us.

"Look at you!" I exclaim, skipping around the car toward him. "You're having so much fun you can't bear to go home yet. Admit it."

His lips turn up slightly and I loop my arm through his. On the back patio, a couple guys are already sitting around drinking and Shaw makes introductions while Zeke gets me, and surprisingly him, another beer.

There are eight of us in total and we sit around a circle in mismatched lawn chairs. A fire pit in the middle lets off just enough warmth to keep the night chill out of the air. Valley days are hot, but the nights get surprisingly cool.

I'm nursing my beer when I glance over and see Zeke's eyes are closed. Reaching out with my foot, I nudge his leg and he opens one eye.

"Why don't you go home and go to bed, old man?" I tease, but my chest tightens with disappointment that he might really leave.

He sits upright. "You ready to go?"

"No, but you obviously are. You can't even keep your eyes open."

"Just tired," he says and runs a hand over his head. It makes the coolest sound as his palm moves back and forth over the short hair.

"So why did you come then?"

"Just looking out for you. Nathan bailed and I don't trust these guys to keep you out of trouble."

"Looking out for me?" I repeat it and mull over his choice of words. It suddenly feels way too hot outside for a fire. "Keep me out of trouble?"

"Yeah, I promised Blair I'd keep an eye on you this week."

My cheeks flame with embarrassment, and I stand and move into the house draining what's left of the warm beer in my hand.

Zeke's loud steps sound behind me. "To be clear, no one forced me to be here tonight or the other night. Blair was just—"

I face off with him, arms crossed over my chest, and he stops talking. "I don't need a babysitter." But... lemons meet lemonade. If he wants to be my chaperone, then so be it. "But, since you're on duty, I need your help."

He doesn't move as I ransack the bathroom and return with two rolls of toilet paper. I hold them out and ask, "Any other bathrooms in the house? Upstairs maybe?"

"Stocking up?"

"No, silly, we're going to TP them."

He shakes his head and takes a step back. "Uh-uh."

"Come on. It'll be awesome." I stick my bottom lip out, but unsurprisingly Zeke doesn't react to my adorable pouty expression except to shake his head again.

"Fine. I'll do it myself." I march out of the house and to the front. Looking around at the houses and the cars driving by, my nerves arrive to the scene. I make a mental plan, complete with design aesthetic, and am just about to move to action when I hear the front door open and close behind me. The smile on my face can't be helped.

"Good. I'm going to need your height," is all I say as I hand him a roll.

"This is a bad idea."

"Oh, lighten up. It's just a little toilet paper."

I lead us to the tallest tree in the yard, a mesquite that's bent and curved toward the neighbor's house. "Lift me up."

I expect more excuses when his hands are suddenly at my hips, lifting me as if I weigh nothing. I falter with the roll in my hand.

"Any day now."

"I don't know what to do," I admit.

My body is hoisted higher and then my ass makes contact with his shoulder.

"Unroll it a bit." I do as he instructs, and he nods. "That's it. Now hold the free end and toss the roll."

I'm frozen, feeling unsure. Maybe he was right. This might be a terrible idea.

"If anyone asks, I'm denying I had anything to do with this." He lets his roll go and it sails through the air in a perfect arc around one of the highest branches and then comes down the other side as my laughter echoes into the night.

Zeke

It takes her three tries to get the toilet paper around the tree. Her aim and power are god awful, but the giggle and smile that accompany her efforts make a perfect beeline to the left side of my chest.

She's reckless and naïve. So desperate to make a mark on the world she doesn't realize she already has. Everybody likes her. The guys think she's hot, of course, but it's nothing as shallow as her looks – it's just her.

Gabby squeals and then covers her mouth to keep quiet.

"You're going to draw attention to us," I whisper.

I'm not really afraid of getting caught. The baseball

guys aren't going to stumble on us unless someone makes a beer run and every house on this street is occupied by college kids. Still, I play along because that's what Gabby is really after with this prank. She wants to feel the adrenaline and rush of doing something sneaky and wrong. The girl couldn't be on the other side of right. I don't think it's in her to be anything but pure and good.

"One more good throw. Aim high."

Focused, she pulls her bottom lip between her teeth and cranks her arm back. When she lets it go, the toilet paper meets its mark and the last of the roll unravels.

Lifting her arms in victory, the shift in weight momentarily causes me to lose my grip and we both overcorrect at the same time. Her body slides down until we're chest to chest. Hers rises and falls, eyes gleaming in the moonlight with mischief and excitement. I'm frozen, body tensed and heart battering in my chest like I finished a workout.

"Now what?" she rasps.

Her words bring me back to reality and I set her on the ground. We step back and eye our handiwork.

"We go back inside and pretend to be shocked when someone notices."

The guys barely glance in our direction as we rejoin them. They're deep in sports talk, which might normally interest me, but the grin that Gabby can't keep off her face keeps pulling me to look at her. She's chomping at the bit for them to find out.

I lean over and whisper, "Want me to make an excuse to leave and come back so I can stumble upon our handiwork all surprised-like?"

Her eyes get big with possibility and I'm wondering when exactly I went from keeping an eye out for her to being a co-conspirator, when Stephens – the catcher for the baseball team – waddles out onto the patio, pants down to his ankles, holding a towel around his waist.

"What the—" Shaw asks, seeing him before the rest of the guys.

Stephen's eyes are wide with panic and mistrust. "Dude. Who the fuck took all the toilet paper?"

eleven

Gabby

"I'm perfectly capable of keeping myself entertained for a week."

Blair's sunburnt face looks remorseful as I deliver the beginning line of my rehearsed guilt trip.

"I know, I'm sorry. I just felt bad I was leaving you. You haven't gone out much by yourself yet."

The truth is I haven't gone out by myself at all until she left for the week, but I'm glad she softened the blow. The rest of my rebuttal falls silent because I know Blair had good intentions and I could never stay mad at her. She doesn't have a mean bone in her body.

"I forgive you, but no more setting up babysitters for me. I left two overprotective parents at home; I don't need another."

"Deal." She leans back in a beach chair and the sound

of the wind whipping around her makes her next line hard to hear. "So, what have you been up to this week?"

"Work, mostly, and hanging out with Nathan. Oh, and I convinced Zeke to help me TP the baseball house."

"Where do you come up with these things? And also, really? Zeke did that?"

I smile, picturing the gleam in his eye as we tossed the toilet paper rolls up into the tree. He was having fun. I doubt he'd admit it, but I saw it.

"It really didn't take a lot of convincing. I just told him I was doing it with or without him. Actually, I have you to thank. You told him to look out for me and in true Zeke fashion, he's given it more dedication than necessary. Especially since you asked. Everyone knows he likes you better than anyone else."

She rolls her eyes, but her smile is pleased. "Well, go easy on him."

"No way," I say with a laugh. "If he wants to act as my protector then I've got plenty of items on my list that I could use back up for."

"Oh God, I've created a monster."

Wes appears on screen, dropping a kiss to Blair's forehead and settling into the chair next to her. "Hey, Gabby."

"Hello." I wave at my best friend's boyfriend. They're too cute together.

"Heard you left Stephens in quite the predicament last night."

My cheeks burn with a mixture of pride and embarrassment for poor Stephens. Blair shoots Wes a confused glance and he fills her in.

"Noooo!" Her eyes go wide as he gets to the end of the story, which he recites with surprising accuracy considering he heard it secondhand. "How did they know it was you?"

"You know I have a terrible poker face."

She nods. "You really do."

"Anyway, Zeke and I had to make an emergency run to the store for toilet paper and beer. I probably have to steer clear of the baseball house for a few days. Good thing Stephens graduates this year. I'm permanently on his shit list."

Wes chuckles. "Shit list."

I head to the Valley student workout facility, which is conveniently located in Ray Fieldhouse – the same facility all the student-athletes use. They have their own fancier, from what I'm told, workout room, but there's always jocks roaming around the building, so it's extra motivation to hit the gym a few times a week.

After the accident, I had to do a lot of therapy – physical and mental – and keeping up with it has become an important part of my progress.

Today I'm here for another reason and it has to do with progressing my social health. I need to get out more – meet new people and not rely on Blair and her social circle. Don't get me wrong, I love hanging with her crowd, but aside from Nathan, they don't feel like my friends yet.

With Nathan on my mind, I decide to check in with him as I warm up on the stair stepper.

Me: Hey, party animal, you alive?
Nathan: Barely. Sorry about last night. Heard you had fun though.

Me: You're forgiven, but you owe me.

Nathan: Done. What are you doing today?

Me: Working tonight.

Nathan: Cool. Wanna hang after?

Me: Maybe. I'll text you when I get off and see if you're awake.

Nathan: I'll be awake.

I do cardio and then wander around the free weights section, eavesdropping on the conversations around me. Two girls are doing sit-ups side by side.

"Wallace totally likes you. I think he's just shy," the girl on the right, a busty redhead with her hair in two long braids says as she pauses at the top of her exercise.

Her friend looks around before asking, "Do you think Madison is more his type? I overheard her talking about how he liked her last selfie."

"Please. Madison is an Insta ho. If you posted pictures where the only thing covering your body was a strategically placed Anatomy textbook, he'd be liking your posts, too."

Note to self, find this Madison's profile. Even I'm intrigued, I can hardly blame poor Wallace.

I have my nicest 'please friend me' smile on as I continue to mosey through the gym. Look, I know other people have already coupled off and friended up, but can't they see the "Friends Wanted" sign flashing above my head? Why is making friends so hard?

A group of girls in purple Tri Sigma shirts walk through the gym, making everyone turn and watch. They've got that, 'we know we're hot walk' down pat. I wonder if they can teach me that walk or if it's like a secret handshake only for members.

The girl in the front of the pack is bouncing with every step, her ponytail swinging from side to side. "Join us outside in fifteen minutes for our monthly fitness class. Don't let spring break throw you off your fitness goals!" she shouts as they exit the room.

I check my reflection in the mirror above the weights and adjust my ponytail. Turning my face to the side, I pull a few wisps forward to help cover the scars. Head held high and with a confidence that is completely fake, I walk out of the weight room and head toward the student-athlete only section. I need to go to that fitness class. I'm certain I can find a new friend out there, but there's only one way I'm going and that's with backup.

My pulse is racing when I approach the basketball court and hear the faint sound of a ball echoing off the floor. Is it possible to feel someone's presence? I'm certain I can even before I turn the corner. And there he is looking like the all-American athlete he is.

I stand on the edge of the sideline, watching him,

totally captivated by the way he moves. He's a different person when he has the basketball in his hands.

"Didn't anyone tell you it's spring break?" I ask as I walk onto the court.

Up close, I can see the sweat.

"That's all anyone seems to be telling me this week." He lifts his shirt to wipe his face and I don't even pretend not to notice the way his abs are cut and practically goading me to reach out and trace the lines where individual muscles separate. "What are you doing here?"

"Recruiting a friend."

One dark brow raises.

"There's a fitness class outside and I want to go, but I don't want to go alone."

"What kind of fitness class?"

"I don't know. Does it matter? I need a workout buddy and here you are." I grab his hand and pull, but he stays rooted to the spot and I fling back like a bungee cord.

I drop his big paw so I can plant my hands on my hips. "If only Blair were here, I'm sure she'd go with me." I pull on the hem of my tank top so the neckline falls below the scoop of my sports bra and the cleavage I'd been hiding on my friendship quest is front and center. I steal a glance down and the girls are as perked up as I am. I can hardly blame them after that ab display. "I guess I'll just roam the halls until I find someone else who will go with me. Can you point me in the direction of the boy's locker room?"

I know just mentioning Blair will do the trick. Zeke has proven time and again that he is annoyingly loyal. I threw the boob display in for dramatic flair, but holy smoke, batman, my ego is getting a nice boost as his heated gaze drops to my chest before he catches himself and looks away. Zeke is a boob guy. Interesting. I file that away in the very short list of things I know about him.

"Fine. Let's go. I still need to do some flexibility training before I call it a day."

I bounce beside him as we walk through the fieldhouse, backtracking the way I came to the general fitness room and out the way the Sigma girls went.

At the first sight of the purple shirts, Zeke's steps slow. "Sweet baby…"

"Goats!" I squeal. "Oh my God, it's goat yoga!" I read the sign and look at the girls sprawled out on their mats, goats roaming between them.

"Hello!" the bouncy leader from earlier greets us in front of the fenced-in area where the goats, and the yogis already in there petting my new furry friends, are hanging out. "Welcome. I'm Misty. We're so happy you could join us." Her head tips up, traveling the length of Zeke's body until she reaches his face. I'm irrationally perturbed that she's checking him out right in front of me. How does she not see that we're together? I'm about to cross her off my future friend list when she flips her head to the side and brings her eyes back to me, giving me the same appraisal.

"I love that sports bra! Does it have back clasps too, or is the zipper the only thing keeping it on?" She steps closer to get a better look.

"Oh, uh." I lift the scoop of my tank back up to cover myself. "Just the zipper. One swift pull and out they pop." I laugh awkwardly and make the sound of a zipper and then an explosion like my boobs are the bomb.

Zeke makes a choked sound and then coughs. When Misty and I look over, he raises his hands and ducks his head. "Sorry. Swallowed wrong."

Misty glances between us and then turns sideways, lifting a hand like Vanna White. "Go on in and find a mat. The class will start in just a few minutes."

"Oh my God, Zeke, they have on horns and wings!"

There are five or six baby goats in total, most of them playing in the middle where a group has gathered to coo and pet them, but in the far corner a small black and brown goat is laying on an empty mat. I hustle in that direction, slip off my shoes and kneel in front of my new best friend.

"Look at him! Oh my goodness. He's so cute."

"She." A woman wearing a Got Goats? t-shirt appears out of nowhere and hands me a piece of animal cracker. "That there is Trixie."

"Hi, Trixie." I run my hand down her back and place the other, palm out, just under her mouth. I glance at Zeke, hovering off to the side like he wants no part of this. "Get over here and meet Trixie."

"I'm good," he says. "Are you okay now? Can I head back?"

"What? No! We're doing goat yoga."

He shakes his head adamantly.

"Come on! It's yoga with GOATS!" I lift Trixie and hold her out to Z who takes a step back. "No thanks."

"Zeke Sweets, are you afraid of a baby goat?"

"Negative. I just don't want to touch it."

I'm two seconds from forcing Trixie into his arms

when Misty claps her hands and moves to the center of the pen. "Grab a mat everyone, we're going to get started."

"Have fun." Zeke backtracks, weaving in and out of mats.

"Oh, there you are, Zeke," Misty calls and motions him over. She looks to the class and exclaims, "Everyone, we have Valley U basketball star Zeke Sweets here with us today." Zeke smiles sheepishly and waves. He looks like he's about to tell her he's leaving, but Misty keeps laying it on thick. "Thank you so much for coming today. It really means a lot to have the support of the student-athlete population. Let's give him a round of applause."

Ever seen a seven-foot man try to disappear into the ground? That's the look Zeke has on his face as thirty girls clap and cheer for him – like he wants the earth to swallow him whole.

I do my best to keep my face neutral as he walks back to the empty mat beside me and takes a seat, but when he leans over, pets Trixie, and says, "You so owe me." I can't help but laugh.

twelve

Zeke

"Thank you for coming with me," Gabby says as we leave the goats and the weirdest hour of my life behind.

"You owe me. That was… I have no words."

"When you post that photo of us with Trixie and her brother standing on our backs while we did the tabletop pose and get nine billion new followers, my debt will be paid in full." She tries to say it with sass, but the usual Gabby spunk isn't quite there.

"You alright?"

"Yeah, of course. That was amazing. Whoever thought up goat yoga is a genius."

She goes silent again and I find myself in the unusual position of feeling like I need to make small talk.

"I didn't know you worked out at the field house."

She nods.

"I also had no idea they had fitness classes out on the yard. Let alone goat yoga. The guys are going to give me so much shit."

"Mhmmm."

We're standing in the hall just outside of the workout room. She has no reason to follow me any farther and I'm not quite ready to leave her alone. Something is off. Call it Blair instincts or Gabby radar, but something is bugging her.

"Are you sure you're okay?"

"I'm fine. Really. It's stupid."

"Did I do something wrong?"

She expels a heavy breath. "No. It's just... I came here today hoping to find some new friends and I just realized I failed spectacularly. Those goats were so adorable I forgot my mission."

I'm processing the words, trying to understand why she'd be looking for friends when she already has a whole bunch of them when she adds, "Blair and her friends are great, but they're her friends. I don't really have any of my own friends yet and I have no idea how to make them." She looks up and groans. "Oh God. Saying it out loud made me realize just how pitiful it sounds." She smiles the biggest, fakest smile. "I've gotta get going. Thanks, Zeke."

I can't think of what to say to stop her, so I head back to the gym. I lay on the floor; head resting on the cool wood and pull out my phone. I scan through the photos and find the one she mentioned. Misty perfectly captured the two seconds both goats stayed still on our backs. Gabby is turned toward me with a real smile on her face – the only kind that belongs there.

Without Gabby to help me, I'm a little slower, but I manage to upload the photo and caption it myself: When your friends trick you into hanging out with goats. The hashtags are impossible, but I go with the obvious #goats #yoga #goatyoga #valleyu and hoping it'll bring a smile to her face #yogawithfriends

The next day, I've got an ice pack on my ankle and a massage pillow on my back as I flip through the channels. I went hard today and pushed myself more than even I thought possible. I'm starving, but according to my nutrition plan, I've blown through my calories for the day after this protein drink in my hand.

When I finish it off, I head out to the pool. Gabby lounges in a chair, my earbuds hanging from her ears. I kinda like that she keeps wearing them even though she's been home plenty of times to get her own.

I take the chair next to hers. "Hey."

"Hey, yourself. I was looking for you earlier. Where've you been?"

"Gym."

Nathan speaks from the giant unicorn he's floating on in the pool. "Told you. You owe me ten bucks."

She looks to me with a pout. "Your dedication cost me ten dollars."

"Why were you looking for me?" A rush of energy that I thought was completely depleted after my workout, shoots to the surface and I bounce my leg.

The Tip-Off

She sits up and holds out an earbud in silent invitation. Her hair's wet and skin red from the hours she spent out by the pool. "I had a question," she says as I listen to the music currently playing on Gabby's playlist.

"What's up?"

"I want to get a tattoo and I was wondering if you'd go with me?"

"When are you going?"

She shrugs. "Tomorrow maybe. I work the day shift so I could go afterward."

"Alright, sure. What are you going to get and where?"

She drags a finger down the side of her ribcage and my eyes are entranced with the movement. Even covered by the white one-piece swimsuit, the curve of that soft space is enticing. "I'm still toying around with the words, but I want it here."

I clear my throat and nod. "Yeah. I've been meaning to get some new ink done. I'll call my guy and see if he can get us in."

She shifts so she can better see the tattoos that cover the entirety of my left arm and hand.

"Do you have tattoos anywhere else?" As she speaks, her index finger reaches out and traces the clock on my left forearm. She follows the short hand to the six and then the long hand to the three.

I shake my head and try not to think about how good it feels to have her eyes and hands on me.

"Why not?"

"I promised my mom I wouldn't end up with tattoos all over my body."

She giggles and the smile on my face gets bigger in

response. I love being the reason she laughs.

"Why a clock?" Her hand falls away and she sits back, smiling at me while she waits for a response I don't give her.

"I should get a shower." I hand her back the earbud and as our fingers graze my eyes lock on the touch, on the unseen current that I feel as the tips of her soft fingers meet mine. That feeling is dangerous to everything I've worked for, so I tell myself it isn't real. "I'll text you about tomorrow."

thirteen

Gabby

The tattoo parlor is on the main street of downtown Valley. It's quiet, as all of Valley is, with everyone having fled for spring break. The shop itself is big and clean and Zeke is greeted by the entire place as we enter.

"Couldn't resist one last piece of art before you leave, eh?" an older guy with leathery tanned skin, a grey braid tossed over each shoulder, and ink peeking out from every inch of skin that isn't covered, speaks up first. The others offer some of the same sentiments as each one takes turns shaking the hand of the man next to me.

Zeke takes their admiration and friendliness in stride and doesn't even look like he wants to hide in the corner.

"Brought a friend." Zeke turns to me and I step forward with the bravest face I can muster. "This is

Gabby. She's looking to get something done too."

The older man extends a hand to me. "Van. Nice to meet you."

"You too."

He waves us back and Zeke and I follow him to a room in the back of the shop. The setup reminds me of a doctor's office. A large black leather chair sits in the middle, a desk on one side with a black stool, but there's no cotton balls or throat swabs in place and the pictures on the wall are framed drawings. Everything from a cross to skulls has been beautifully drawn and colored.

"What did you have in mind?" he asks as he motions for me to have a seat. Zeke hangs back, his large frame blocking the entryway. He hovers like he isn't sure if he should stay or go.

I reach into my back pocket before sitting and hand Van the paper. He takes it, has a seat on the stool and smooths out the paper, looking over it for a long moment before speaking. "Did you do the lettering on this?" His grey eyes meet mine and there's a mix of intrigue and admiration there.

I nod.

"It's beautiful. You're very talented."

I manage to mumble my thanks, all too aware of Zeke creeping forward.

"Do you know where you want it?" Van asks.

"On my left side." I point to the spot.

"Hold tight. It'll just take me a few minutes to prep."

As he leaves the room, Zeke comes closer. "Nervous?" he asks.

"Yeah. It hurts, doesn't it?" An anxious laugh escapes.

Zeke cracks a smile. "A little. Want me to go first and show you how it's done?"

"Yes, please." My body relaxes a bit, thankful to have a few more minutes to mentally prepare.

When Van returns, we tell him the change of plans and Zeke gets into the hot seat. Standing on the right side of Zeke, I watch as Van freehands a replica of the red headphones that often are around Z's neck. The placement is on his inner bicep just below a small roadrunner like the Valley mascot. After that piece is done, Van adds a trail of music notes that creeps up to Zeke's shoulder in between the rest of his tattoos. The new ink blends in against Zeke's other artwork creating a beautiful scene of images like a picture book. The story of Zeke Sweets.

"It's perfect," I say as Van finishes and starts to cover the new ink with ointment.

Z stands and both guys look to me.

"Ready?" Van asks.

I can only nod as I get into the chair. Van reclines it until I'm lying flat on my back and then has me turn onto my right side.

"You want me to wait out front?" Zeke asks, taking a step to the door.

I shake my head and with unsteady hands lift the hem of my shirt slowly. I can feel Van behind me, but it's Zeke's heated gaze I avoid.

Van doesn't miss a beat as the scars that cover the left side of my stomach and back are exposed. "How about right here?" he asks and lines up the tracing just below the ugliest red scar that refuses to fade with the others.

"That's good." The emotion and vulnerability in my voice makes it small and high pitched.

I turn my head back to face straight ahead. Zeke steps forward, pulls a chair from the corner of the room and sits beside me. Most people would describe Zeke as quiet, but the way he observes, listens, takes in everything around him is loud and right now, the silence screams.

"You good?"

"A little nervous," I admit.

Van shifts the stencil around. The design touches my scars in two different places and Van lightly runs his fingertip over each of them, causing my body to go still. "Are they sensitive to touch?"

I nod.

"I'll be as gentle as I can, but I won't sugar coat it – tattooing over scars can be pretty painful. You're sure about this?"

"Positive."

"She's tough," Z says, taking one of my hands in his. "Squeeze if it hurts. It'll take your mind off it. Plus, added bonus, you get to inflict pain on me."

I squeeze once as hard as I can and he chuckles, removes his right hand and replaces it with his left. "On second thought, I better give you my weak hand. You break my right hand and Sara'll break my other one and then kick my ass."

His kindness breaks the tension and I give in and look up into his face. I find none of the pity I'd expected. He looks at me like he's always looked at me. His eyes are a light brown full of warmth or hardness depending on his mood. Right now, they are only warmth as he studies my expression.

"Alright, here we go," Van says and the sound of the tattoo gun hums to life.

I close my eyes briefly, but Zeke's voice comes closer. "You got this. Don't think about it."

I open my eyes and roll them. Easier said than done.

The first prick of the gun pulls a moan from my lips and I squeeze Zeke's hand. He returns the pressure and leans down so he's looking only at my face. I let my lids flutter closed again and try and focus on anything but the sting of pain. It's not totally unbearable until he hits the first bit of scar tissue. I gasp and Zeke squeezes my hand harder.

"Oh God," I say quietly.

"Hey, look at me," Zeke orders.

I do my best to look brave as I open my eyes and stare up at him.

"The clock was the first tattoo I ever got." His low voice steals my attention and the pain recedes to the background like the hum of the gun. Something about the way he speaks and the look in his eye makes my heart race. "It reminds me that every day, every second counts. Twenty-four hours, eighty-six thousand four hundred seconds."

"Why six-fifteen?"

He doesn't answer right away. His jaw ticks and I squeeze his hand.

"That's what time it was when my dad walked out of my life."

I try and hide the shock from my face, sure I'm doing a shit job. "That's awful, why would you want to remember that?"

"Because in an instant, my life changed. So did his. He was a movie director. Is a movie director, I guess. He left when I was eleven. Moved to Hollywood to try and make it big. He succeeded too. He became a hotshot Hollywood director and never looked back. It's not about the time, though, it's that at any time things can change on a dime. I don't want to forget that. Every moment counts."

I want to ask so many questions, but he smiles at me and I can't do anything but smile back. He gets it. I've thought of him as being someone who doesn't understand how important it is to seize the day, grab every chance and opportunity by the balls, but that's not true. He is seizing the day – his priorities are just different. I don't know if he has it right or if I do, but maybe it doesn't matter. We're each living our life focused on what's important to us.

"All done here," Van says proudly. "What do you think?" He holds a mirror so I can see the words now inked onto my skin forever.

"I love it."

fourteen

Zeke

*G*abby met me at the tattoo parlor, so we part ways after we've paid and thanked Van. I'd sort of assumed, and maybe hoped, Gabby was planning on coming back to The White House, but she's not here when I get back and an hour later it seems pretty clear she's not coming.

Me: Where you at? Gabby with you?

I scarf down my sixth meal of the day as I wait for Nathan to respond. The house is quiet, so wherever the party is tonight, it's not here and if the party isn't here then neither is Nathan.

Nathan: Nah, Gabby said she didn't feel like coming out tonight. I'm at Shaw's dorm playing

video games.

Well, shit. There could be a million different reasons she didn't feel like going out, but something tells me it has everything to do with the vulnerability and emotion I'd seen on her face at the tattoo shop. She'd been nervous and not just about the pain, but about showing me her scars. And those words she'd chosen to have placed on her body forever, *Beauty in imperfection*. I can't decide if it's supposed to be inspiring or depressing.

I groan into the quiet kitchen. I don't know if I said or did the right thing, maybe this is all my fault. I brace both hands on the counter and replay the night again looking for some inspiration on what to do next.

The back door opens and Gabby steps through, sending my pulse racing. "Hey."

"Hey," I respond, too much eagerness in my voice. I step forward and then force myself to stand still.

"I just need to get my stuff. I left a few things in Wes' room and they get back tomorrow."

She disappears upstairs before I can think what to say and is back just as fast and heading to the door without more than a nod in my direction.

"Hey, wait, you don't have to run off. How's the tattoo? Does it hurt?" I'm well aware I'm rambling, but she stops, so that's all that matters.

Her steps falter and she turns back to face me. "No, not really."

"Let's see." I close the distance between us in two long strides. She lifts her tank, revealing the bandage still covering her new tattoo. My gaze blazes down and I finally let myself take in the scars I tried so very hard not to see earlier.

They're extensive. Some have faded more than others, but each one stands out against the rest of her flawless, smooth skin. She doesn't pull back as I run my thumb just below the bandage. "You can probably take this off now."

She sets her bag on the counter and then starts to peel back the tape, wincing when it pulls the skin.

"Let me." Her fingers drop and I step closer. "The tape is a little tricky. Comes off easiest if you peel from the side. There we go." We both stare down at the fresh blue ink.

"Thank you for holding my hand tonight."

"It was my pleasure, Gabby." I pull a beer from the fridge so I have something to do. "You want something to drink?"

She thinks for a moment and then breezes past me and pulls a bottle of tequila from a cabinet. "I think I'm going to need something stronger than beer."

She finds a glass and pours herself a shot while I lean onto the counter and take a long pull of my beer. "Plans tonight?"

She takes her phone from her front pocket and makes a little humming noise as she glances at it. "No, I don't see anything appealing for tonight."

My face must give away my confusion because she turns her phone so I can see the screen. I take the phone. It's a bulleted list. "Go to a frat party, eat at the campus cafeteria?"

"Don't read them aloud. It's embarrassing." She doesn't reach to stop me but takes the shot, grimaces, and then covers her face with both hands.

"Ah, is this the list of things you want to do now that you're at Valley?" I ask, remembering the mention of it the day after the foam party.

"Yes," she groans. "My pathetic list of things to make me less... well, pathetic."

"Relax," I say as I keep reading. "We've all got things we want to do. It's not embarrassing at all." I believe those words too until I keep reading. My face gets warm and I start to get a very clear picture of why Gabby didn't want me to say them out loud. Go commando stands out, but so does witness a fight, skinny dip, and lose virginity.

She takes the phone from me before I can finish. I need to bleach my eyes, or maybe my brain, so I can look at her without thinking about her doing all that and more.

"What's on your list?" She pours another shot.

"Play in the NBA."

She laughs. "What else?"

I shrug, thinking over the items on her list. I feel a little tinge of sadness that I never thought to make a list for college. Never thought to line up to-dos, never even thought to have things other than ball on any list. One shot. One dream. One chance. Everything else is noise.

"Never? There was never anything else you wanted besides ball?"

"What can I say, I'm a simple guy. Sure, I thought about other things, tried to picture my life going in another direction, but the only time I ever felt complete was with a basketball in my hand."

"That's how finally being at Valley makes me feel. Alive, free, and—"

"Whole," we say at the same time. She smiles at me and I can't resist smiling right back at her. She tips back her second shot, grimacing slightly less this time as the liquor goes down.

"You should do everything on your list then, just maybe wait 'til Blair's back and can keep an eye on you."

She rolls her eyes. "And you should add something to your list that pushes you out of your comfort zone."

"I'm serious."

"Me too. Just one thing. Name one thing you'd like to do that has nothing to do with basketball."

I look up and bring a hand to my chin like I'm in deep concentration then back to her, meeting her fierce blue eyes. "Skinny dipping does sound pretty good."

She grabs the tequila bottle and heads to the back door. "Well, come on then."

Gabby

"I was kidding," I say when Zeke calls my bluff.

We stand by the pool looking down at the clear water.

"Well, I'm not getting in there without you," he says as he takes a seat on the edge of the pool. "Then I'll just be a creepy dude skinny dipping alone."

"I can't get in with my new ink," I say, but the butterflies in my stomach sure wish I could.

We sit together, letting our feet dangle in the warm water.

"You really did the lettering for your tattoo?" he asks.

"I did."

"Van was right. You're really talented." His hand falls to my wrist and he pulls on the end of one of my bracelets. "I know you made these, too. Blair wears hers proudly."

I smile as I look down at the friendship bracelets on my arms. Blair and I have been making and wearing them as long as I can remember. "I had a lot of time over the last few years to try a bunch of different things. Hand lettering, pottery – that one didn't work out as well. I like being creative, though, making beautiful things. Somehow it makes me feel beautiful."

"You don't think you're beautiful?" He shakes his head. "You are one of the most beautiful people I know. You're fun and kind, and—"

I cut him off. "I know, I know. It's what's on the inside that counts. I'm so tired of people telling me that. Is it too much to hope that someone will be able to look past the scars and find me beautiful on the outside too?"

His expression tells me I've said too much, and I apologize. "I shouldn't drink tequila. It removes what little filter I have sober. I'm gonna grab a beer."

Standing, I take the bottle of tequila with me to the kitchen and exchange it for a Bud Light. Clearly, I need to slow down before I get all emotionally slutty. I hear the door open and I turn, expecting Zeke, but instead find my best friend, practically glowing with a golden tan and beachy hair.

"Hey, I thought you weren't getting back until

tomorrow morning."

She drops her bag and squeezes me hard. "We got an early start this morning. Oh my God, I missed you." She pulls back. "You smell like tequila. Are you and Nathan getting drunk together?"

"Not exactly. Zeke and I were just hanging out by the pool."

She looks like she wants to ask more, but I wave her outside. "Come and tell me all about your trip."

The rest of the group joins us, and we sit outside while they fill us in on their vacation. I steal glances at Zeke and each time our eyes meet my pulse quickens.

"So, tell me about what you guys did," Blair asks. The insinuation clear in her expression.

She's sitting on Wes' lap and he drops a kiss to her forehead before saying, "You mean, besides TPing the baseball house and hanging out with the young guys? What the hell, man?"

Zeke shrugs but doesn't answer.

"Speaking of," Joel asks with a wicked smirk, "when do we get more couple pics of Zebby? I'm waiting with breath that is baited to see what my new favorite couple does next. Goat yoga? Priceless!"

I know he's just kidding, but Katrina punches his arm and gives her boyfriend a look to shut it.

Zeke looks uncomfortable at the attention, so I field it. "First of all, Zebby is a terrible couple name. Try again. Secondly, you'll have to follow along with everyone else."

I flash Zeke a smile hoping I haven't made him more uncomfortable, but he grins back and then winks.

The conversation dies off after that and one by one,

the couples announce they're headed to bed.

Blair hugs me tightly. "I really missed you."

"Missed you too."

Wes even comes in for a hug. "You coming with us on the next trip?"

Blair pulls back. "Oh right, I forgot to tell you. We're driving up to the lake next weekend. Are you in?"

"You've been back in Valley for less than two hours and you've already planned another trip?"

"It's a yearly trip," Wes says. "The entire basketball team goes and usually some guys from the baseball team, too. Last trip before graduation. Not even Z can get out of this one."

"So... you'll come, right?"

"I'm probably on the schedule at work," I remind her. I'm seriously starting to regret taking a job that requires me to work weekends.

The next week things start to fall into a routine. I spend my days on campus exploring or holed up in the library to work on my online classes, which Blair finds hilarious because according to her, the perk of online classes is that you don't have to go to campus, but I love it here. The Valley University campus is beautiful and everything I dreamed it would be.

My nights are spent either hanging with Blair or at The Hideout.

On Thursday, I'm rolling silverware and exchanging

funny memes with Nathan via text when Brady approaches. He doesn't look up from his tablet as he says, "Savannah is taking your shifts this weekend."

My stomach knots. "Did I do something wrong? Please don't fire me. I need this job. I like this job." Both statements are true. My parents were supportive of my moving to Valley, but they made it clear they wouldn't be covering my rent.

He looks up after a beat. "You're not fired. You put in a late request to have the weekend off and I'm honoring it. In the future, though, I'd appreciate at least two weeks' notice."

"Yes, of course."

I call Blair as soon as I get home. "What time are we leaving tomorrow?" I ask, pulling out my bag and then scanning my closet for outfits.

"We're leaving as soon as Wes gets done with his one o'clock class."

"Wait. Why don't you sound more surprised that I'm suddenly free? What do you know?"

"You didn't think I was going to let you miss out on this weekend, did you?"

"But how?" I drop to my bed and cross my legs underneath me.

"Zeke talked to Brady. I dunno, I didn't get the details, it doesn't matter. We're going to the lake!"

I put Blair on speaker as she goes on about all the things she wants to do while we're there.

Me: You talked Brady into letting me off this weekend?!

Zeke: If I have to go, you have to go. Besides, we have unfinished business.

Me: ?

Zeke: Skinny dipping of course.

The next day nearly all the basketball team, their girlfriends, and even a few baseball guys pile into five vehicles, with another group coming later. It's a short drive from Valley to the lake, but the outstretch of water makes it feel like a million miles away from the desert landscape of Valley.

"Where's Nathan?" I ask as we split up and claim our rooms in the cabin. There are three cabins in total and each one overlooks the lake. Joel's family owns the one we're staying in and rents the other two for the yearly team gathering.

"He's coming up later," Wes answers as he and Blair put their bags into one of the four rooms upstairs. Joel and Katrina are in the master, Nathan and Zeke are sharing, and I get a room all to myself, though I'm sandwiched between the two couples so I'm not sure I should celebrate my good fortune just yet.

We head out for a quick spin on the boat so Joel can show us all the hot spots and then everyone comes over to our cabin. Joel's got the grill going and the guys hang around helping, but mostly just talking smack, while the girlfriends and I huddle around the outdoor bar talking about them.

The rest of the girls are commiserating over travel schedules and long practices that keep their boyfriends occupied. I know from Blair that dating an athlete means they're gone or practicing a lot, but it seems like the moments Blair and Wes do have together they more than make up for his absence. I could get on board with that.

I stop listening but give the appropriate head nods and "mhmms" with the rest of the group. Across the deck, Zeke stands just on the outside of the guys' circle looking as bored with the conversation as me.

I get his attention, which isn't hard since our eyes seem to constantly be snagging, and motion with my head for him to follow me. I slowly back away from the girls and head to the stairs that lead down to the lake. Zeke meets me on the bottom stair.

"Is it time for the skinny dipping already?" he teases.

"Even better."

On the dock, I stop next to a jet ski. Zeke looks from it to me and back. "You know how to drive that thing?"

"I saw Joel start it earlier."

He watches me as I stow my cell phone in a cabinet and then ease myself down onto the jet ski, crossing his arms over his chest, an amused expression on his face.

"Well, come on. I need an accomplice."

He tosses me a life jacket and I put it on. Good call. "More like a chaperone." His weight rocks the jet ski and I hold on tight until he gets settled behind me. "Maybe I should drive."

"No way." My hands shake as I focus on the controls trying to remember the exact steps Joel took.

"You good?"

"I got this."

fifteen

Zeke

We putter around the lake. There's really no other way to describe the way she drives. Gabby, a slow driver? I did not expect that. She goes all out in every other aspect of her life.

Her expression is all determination and focus as she steers the jet ski. Slowly the speed increases and just when I think we're going to go more than ten miles per hour, she backs off. Again.

My arms are draped loosely around her waist, but at her hesitation, I move my hands to cover hers on the handlebars. She relinquishes control easily but doesn't move her hands as I increase the speed and navigate us around the lake. Sensing her unease, I keep it a little slower than I'd go if I were by myself.

The longer we ride, the more tension eases from her

shoulders and her body leans back into mine. After we've circled the lake, I drive us back to the cabin, stopping and letting us idle before returning to our friends.

"It's really beautiful out here," she says, dropping her arms. She angles her body to the side, giving me a better view of her as she takes in the lake. "I could stay here forever."

"Yeah, it's pretty nice, but we should probably get back before they send out a search party. Joel is monitoring my fun this weekend to make sure I'm having the appropriate amount."

"And are you, having the appropriate amount?"

"Yeah, it's cool being up here."

"But?"

"How do you know there's a but?"

She arches a brow.

"*But*, it's bad timing. I don't have a lot of time left before the draft. Sara wants me to drop some weight, be more on target with the weight of a typical NBA center and I'm trying to stay sharp, keeping up with my workouts and drills."

"I get that. You're so close and you want to do everything you can, but you've gotta enjoy these moments." Her tone is wistful, and her features inspired as she looks out to the water and the blue sky that stretches into the mountains. "After the accident when I was sitting up in my room too embarrassed to face my friends because of the scars, it was moments like this that I missed the most. I'd fantasize about hanging out and just being, no cares in the world. When it's all said and done, it's the human interaction you remember the most. Personal goals, awards, they don't mean anything without people to share them with." She turns to look at me. "When you're a big NBA star traveling around the country with fans screaming and paparazzi everywhere, you're going to miss this."

My throat is thick as I swallow. "I think you're right about that."

Her smile widens. Blonde hair blowing like a halo around her, skin sun-kissed, eyes the color of the water you see in those commercials for vacations where you stay in the little huts. Before I do something stupid like kiss her, I turn to watch a boat pass by, giving them a small wave.

"How's the list going?" My voice comes out gruff and I clear it before I continue. "Check off online dating yet?" My chest is tight while I wait for her response. Picturing her hooking up with some asshole who doesn't know how amazing she is, makes me want to keep her out here on this jet ski forever.

"I can't bring myself to respond to any of the messages. I don't think it's for me. I kept the profile, though. The pickup lines are a nice boost to my ego." She laughs. "Wanna hear the worst one?"

I nod.

"Can I follow you where you're going right now? Because my parents always told me to follow my dreams!"

"Damn, that's awful."

She grins and we fall silent. I feel her sigh before I hear it. "Alright, fine, we can go back now."

On our walk back from the dock to the cabin, she grabs my hand and swings our arms playfully between us. I stop, tug her hand so she has to stop too. "Before we go back. I, uh, made you a playlist."

Gabby started following my music account after that first night we listened to music together and we've texted a few times about it, prompting me to create my new lists with more than just myself in mind.

"You did?" Her voice is excited and surprised. She pulls out her phone like she's going to check it out now.

"Listen to it later," I urge and pull her toward our friends.

Gabby returns to the girls, and I head over to where the guys are. Joel shoves a beer in my hand, like the dude has been waiting for me to return. "How's the fun level?" he asks, raises his hand to his head and then gives me a thumbs up. I crack a smile, shake my head, and open the beer.

As the night goes on, I do start to have more fun, relax as the alcohol gets in my system, and try and remember Gabby's words from earlier. She's right. These moments are almost done and, yeah, I need to keep busting my ass as I work toward the draft and my pro rookie season, but this may be the last time I get to hang with all my teammates before graduation.

Joel sits beside me, Katrina on his lap. The couples have all started to pair off as the sun sets and the stars come out. Gabby sits in a chair by herself, feet pulled up, hugging her bare legs.

"No way," Joel's voice cuts through all the chatter on the deck and I look up to see Shaw and Nathan joining us.

"Dude, what did you do to your head?" someone calls out.

Nathan's trademark long locks have been buzzed off and his hair is cropped short to his head. It's not his hair that has me sitting up straight and swallowing down a lump that's forming in my throat, it's the way Gabby is on her feet and running toward him, throwing her arms around his neck and then pulling back and running her fingers through his hair.

I'm jealous. It's such a foreign feeling it takes a minute to identify the unused emotion. I've always gone after what I wanted with no apologies. And I was successful more times than not. I never wanted anything I couldn't have, but I want her, and I can't have her.

Relationships are a distraction and it's never been more critical that I keep focused than now when I'm so close. Is it possible to juggle the NBA and be in a relationship? Maybe. But is it really worth the risk to find out?

sixteen

Gabby

"What did you do?" I run my fingers through Nathan's short hair. It's got a little curl to it, something I had not expected, and I can't stop touching it. "And when and why?"

"You like it?"

"I love it. I can see your face now."

He blushes and an embarrassed smile tugs at his lips. "Thanks."

Nathan's grand entry has spurred everyone to get up and move around and Joel announces he's going to take the boat out for a night drive. I follow Nathan down to the dock with some of the other guys who hadn't gone out earlier. I look around for a certain tall, dark, and handsome man, but he's nowhere to be found. A group of guys went in to play cards and Zeke must have gone with them. Or maybe his fun meter tapped out and he went to bed.

The boat roars to life and the wind whips through my hair. A shiver makes my whole body shake and Nathan wraps an arm around me sharing his heat with me. The houses lit up around the lake like a postcard and the gentle waves of the water as we cruise around has us all quiet and soaking up the moment.

I close my eyes, so tired and satiated from the day. It was absolutely perfect. I mentally cross weekend at the lake off my list but then add it right back because I want more weekends just like this.

"Gabs baby, wake up." Nathan's voice whispers as he runs a hand down my arm.

When I open my eyes, we're the last two people on the boat and docked back at Joel's cabin.

"Guess I was tired," I say, a little mortified as I pull my head from his chest. I wonder how long I was passed out cold and hopefully I didn't drool on him.

"It happens. Days out on the water with sun and beer take it out of you."

I stand up and stretch, take a step to get off the boat and he grabs my hand. "Wait."

He's still seated and pulls me so that my knees are enclosed by his. "I, uh… wanted to talk to you before we go back."

It takes a moment for my foggy brain to decipher the look in his eye and the way his thumb gently strokes my wrist. I'm caught so off guard I give my head a little shake, certain I'm dreaming this whole thing up. There's never been anything but friendship between Nathan and me. Our friendship has been easy and comfortable – not the things of great love, or even great lust, stories. Or at least not from my perspective. The way he looks at me right now though, I think I've missed something.

"We're friends, right?" I ask. He nods and the way his face falls, I feel awful for not realizing he felt differently sooner. "I don't know what I would do without you."

"It's okay," he says. "I get it."

"No, you don't." I sit next to him. "The past month has been crazy. I was scared out of my mind, but every step of the way, you've been there. No one has been there for me more than you." It's only after I've said the words that I realize it's not exactly true. Zeke's been there for me more than anyone. Forced or not, it's true. Blair, who will always be more like a sister than a friend, but she's wrapped up with Wes and her own life. Nathan is a great friend, but he's not always been there when I needed him. It's been Zeke at every turn. "We're friends. We're *good* as friends."

"Yeah, you're right." He lets out a long breath. "I don't know what I was thinking. I'm such an idiot."

"Hey," I nudge his knee with mine. "You're not."

"No, I am. Trust me on that."

"You can talk to me. You know that, right? You've taken care of me the past month, but I'm here for you too. Any time."

"Thanks, Gabs."

Back at the cabin we part, a little awkwardness still lingering. The last thing I want is for things to be weird with Nathan. I track down Blair and Vanessa inside and slump down onto the sofa between them.

"Hey, you," Vanessa says coyly. "Where have you

been?"

"On the boat with Nathan." I let my head fall back.

"And?" Blair asks.

"Did Nathan finally make a play?" Vanessa adds.

I lift my head up and look to each of their smiling faces. "You two knew?"

Their laughter has me shaking my head.

"He cut his hair because of you! You said you liked short hair and voila!"

"No." But as I say the word, I think back to the kitchen when I'd told him, and everyone else, that I preferred short hair. "I dunno. I honestly had no idea he thought of me like that at all."

"We know," they say in unison.

Blair squeezes my hand. "Are things going to be okay between the two of you? I know how close you two have become."

"Yeah." I nod. "I think so."

"So now that Nathan has professed his feelings, who will be next?" Vanessa smirks. "You've turned into quite the little heartbreaker."

My cheeks flush at her teasing and I smile, wishing that were true. "Have you guys seen Zeke around? He was going to help me with one of the items on my list."

"Which item, Gabriella?" Blair bats her lashes. "Virginity?"

Vanessa's eyes go wide. "I don't know what list she's referring to, but it sounds fun."

I stand and shake my head at them.

"Anal?" Vanessa shouts after me.

The Tip-Off

Zeke

Gabby: Meet me at the dock

From my seat at the dining room table, currently covered in cards and poker chips, I can see the path down to the dock, but the dock itself is dark so I can't tell if she's already there.

"Raise," Datson says and lobs three black chips into the center.

I look at my hand one last time as if I'm truly considering it and toss them down. "Fold." I push back from the table. "Deal me out."

"Lame," Joel calls out. He places his hand over his head and then turns it into a thumbs down.

I can't make out her form until I'm halfway down to the water. She sits on the dock, feet dangling above the water. She's so fucking beautiful and innocent and I want to ruin her and worship her all at the same time. I'm not going to do either of those things, though. I'm going to stick to the path. The path doesn't include dating. The path doesn't even include fun most days and Gabby deserves days that are all about fun.

She turns her head as I get closer and there's that big Gabby smile pointed right at me. "Hey."

"Hey, yourself. Whatcha doing down here all alone?"

"I thought we could cross skinny dipping off both our lists."

My brows raise. "What about your tattoo?"

She shrugs. "It's been a week. I'm willing to risk a quick dip if you are."

I rub a hand over my chin. I'm not ashamed of my body, but I'd also prefer not to have my black ass photographed if one of my teammates happen to stumble upon us. Last year one of the sophomores got drunk at a party and passed out naked in the bathroom. I have no idea why he was naked in there, but the photos of his hairy ass were everywhere. My ass is baby smooth and awesome, but I still don't want it on display.

"Well, come on before someone sees us." She's unbuttoning her shorts and pushing them down while I stand there gawking. The sight of her bare legs puts me in motion. Just not a part of me I want in motion right now. I turn around, give my dick a little pep talk that includes promises I won't be a celibate asshole forever, and then undress to my boxers.

"You decent?" I ask over my shoulder.

"No. Oh my God, don't look." She laughs, I hear her footsteps on the dock and then a splash. A few seconds later, she calls, "Your turn."

I push my boxers down and then hold my hands over my junk, semi-erect still because promises be damned, and take two large steps before jumping in beside her. Her happy squeals direct my entry into the lake as I clear the water from my eyes. We're treading water buck naked not two feet from one another. It's a little trippy. I haven't spent time with a girl naked like this in... well forever. If I'm naked and this close to a girl, it's for one purpose and though I'm a gentleman, of course, it's not about anything but carnal desires being met. Thrusts and grunts and release.

I don't think it would be like that with Gabby. No, I *know* it wouldn't be like that, which is another reason it can't happen.

"So now what?" she asks, suddenly looking a little nervous.

"Far as I know, this is all there is to it. How do you feel?"

"Naked." She laughs. "But also like a rebel."

She splashes water at me playfully and I do it right back.

"Think anyone can see us?"

I shrug. "Maybe. Do you want them to see you?"

"God, no," she says too fast. The excitement in her eyes is a dead giveaway. I think Gabby likes the thrill, the possibility of being caught, and God help me because I want nothing more than to keep her safe while she explores every sordid fantasy.

I'm lost in ideas that I'll never act on when she swims toward the dock. "We should probably get out. Don't want to ruin Van's work."

I turn while she pulls herself up out of the water.

"All clear."

When I face her, she's dressed, shirt clinging to her still damp skin, and her long, wet hair shines under the moonlight.

"Can you grab my phone for me?" I ask and point to my stack of clothes. "It's in the front pocket of my shorts."

She looks apprehensive but does as I ask, bringing

the phone to me and placing it in my outstretched hand.

"Lean down here and take a picture with me. Gotta capture the moment."

She snorts, smiles, and bends down as I angle the camera to fit us into the frame. I've never taken a selfie before but turns out it's easy with my long arms and Gabby's beautiful face. I snap a couple and then hand the phone back to her.

After she deposits it on top of my clothes, she asks, "Was that your first selfie?"

"That obvious?"

She giggles. "Is that for your adoring fans?"

"Nah, that was for me."

I pull myself out of the water and she takes a seat back on the dock, facing away from me and giving me privacy without my asking. Once I'm dressed, I join her, phone in hand.

I glance down at the pictures, opening them one by one and then stopping on my favorite. Her smile is biggest in this one and she looks so happy and relaxed. She'd tilted her head toward mine so the left side of her face is hidden. I sort of hate that. I hate that even in a post skinny dipping selfie where she'd just bared herself of clothing and modesty she'd already thought to hide her scars.

"I like this one," I say and hold it out for her approval.

She nods and plays with the frayed hem of her shorts. "You should post it. It won't be goat yoga popular, but it's pretty close."

"Yeah, alright." I pull up my social media and upload the picture. "Got any suggestions for hashtags on this one?"

She takes my phone and types the caption, Late night swim at the lake with friends #collegedays #daysonthelake #nightswim #friendshipgoals #skinnydipping #seizetheday

There are about a dozen more hashtags, but my attention focuses on the last one. Seize the day.

seventeen

Gabby

$\mathcal{S}$aturday goes by in a blur. We go out on the boat, take turns on the jet skis, have lunch on the other side of the lake at a little spot that has live music and an outdoor bar, and then come back to the cabin for a nap with plans to go out as a group tonight.

I haven't seen much of Nathan or Zeke. They both stayed back at the cabin today. Nathan was still sleeping when we left, and Zeke opted out so someone else could go on the boat.

I set the alarm on my phone for thirty minutes before the agreed meetup time and climb into bed fully clothed. I'm about to turn on my sleeping playlist when I remember Zeke said he'd made a new one for me.

I'm humming with anticipation as I scroll through Zeke's playlists, skimming titles for one that might be new, uncertain what I'm looking for exactly but hoping I'll know it when I see it. As it turns out, I do. At the very bottom of the list is one I've never seen before and his labeling makes it clear this one is for me. *For Gabby.* Concise and to the point.

When I open my playlist, my gaze snags on the subtitle, *You're beautiful on the outside too.* My heart is pounding as I scan the list of songs. Each one has the word beautiful, sexy, hot, gorgeous, and my personal favorite, bootylicious, in the title.

When I press play and Snoop Dogg's "Beautiful" plays, I laugh and sigh and swoon all at the same time. It's the nicest and most thoughtful thing anyone has ever done for me. And wait, Zeke thinks I'm beautiful? I don't play it cool for even a second as I open my texts and send him a message to verify the new information.

Me: You think I'm beautiful?

He doesn't respond until the fourth song is playing and I'm hanging on every word of "Beautiful" by Bazzi like Zeke is singing it to me himself.

Zeke: Found the playlist, huh?

Zeke: Yes, Gabby, I think you're beautiful.

I give a little squeal and then remember he's staying in the same cabin and quite possibly within hearing distance.

Me: What are you doing right now?

Zeke: At the driving range with some of the guys.

Me: Are you going out tonight?

Zeke: Yes. It's non-negotiable fun according to Joel.

Zeke: What are you up to?

Me: Getting ready to nap and listening to my playlist.

Zeke: Enjoy, beautiful girl

eighteen

Zeke

*N*athan takes a cut, his ball hooks to the left, and he swears under his breath.

"Think that haircut took your chill 'tude with it," Wes says.

"I can't believe you cut your hair just to get friend-zoned." Shaw chuckles as he steps up to the tee, pulling his driver cold like he knows what he's doing.

"Yeah, well how was I supposed to know Zebby was real."

My head snaps up at one of the many couple names Joel has been trying out in reference to me and Gabby. "What?"

Nathan shoves his golf club into the bag and stalks off toward the clubhouse without answering.

"Did I miss something?" I ask and look to the guys.

Wes lets out a sigh. "He likes Gabby and I think he might be a little pissed with all the attention Gake or Zebby, or whatever your couple name is, getting after you posted that photo last night."

"Shit. I had no idea."

"He'll get over it." Shaw dismisses it with a wave of his hand and takes a generous swing, shanking the ball.

I go after Nathan, not entirely sure what I'm going to say or do when I catch him. He finds his words before I do. "Let me guess, you had no idea and you're sorry?"

I falter. "I didn't and I am."

His jaw tightens as the bartender slides a beer in front of him. "Can I get one of those too?" I ask and place enough cash on the bar to cover both drinks.

We sit in silence until I've got my beer in hand.

"Sorry, man, I really didn't know."

He stares at me with hurt and anger flashing in his blue eyes. "Yeah, I know. You never do. You've got big things on the horizon and you're laser-focused. We all know, man. It's the same excuse every time you skip out on a party or forget someone's birthday. 'That's just Z, he's going to the NBA.' Like that gives you a pass for not giving a shit about anyone but yourself."

"Not give a shit? I've saved your ass more times than I can count. Carried you home when you were too wasted to walk, stopped you from going postal in the middle of the night. Don't tell me I haven't been there."

His eyes flare and he takes another swallow of his beer and then stands. "Gabby is a cool chick and she and I were probably never going to happen anyway, but if you break her heart, I will not hesitate to punch you in the face. I don't care how many times you think you've saved my ass."

By the time we get to the bar later that night, Nathan's mood seems to have bounced back. Mine has not. The more I think about what he said, the more I wonder if he's right.

Gabby springs toward where I sit at the outside bar. It's a huge place with three bars in total. One outside, and two inside on each of the two levels.

"Come with us upstairs," she urges, looping her arm through Nathan's. "There's a dance floor that overlooks the water."

"I don't think so."

"Come on." Her voice pleads and I look to Nathan hoping he'll give me some sign what to do.

He stops a waitress carrying a tray of shots and gets three, handing one to Gabby and then me in some sort of alcoholic peace offering.

"To the last hurrah before graduation," he says, lifting his, and Gabby and I follow suit.

I nod my thanks. "To the last hurrah."

An excited Gabby leads the way upstairs where, sure enough, the music is even louder, and people are dancing on a balcony that overlooks the stage outside and the water just beyond. Shaw and Cannon are chatting up some girls near the bar.

Once I follow Gabby to the dance floor, I look back to see Nathan has gone off to join them, leaving us alone. But not for long because Gabby spots Wes, Joel, and Mario and of course their girlfriends and dances toward them. Flashbacks to the night of the foam party where we had this very same setup come to mind.

Mario leans in but still has to shout to be heard over the music. "Heard you went skinny dipping last night."

I nod. "Guess I did."

"What are you two up to tonight and should I alert the paparazzi? Some naked photos of you might be just the boost you need to get that top draft spot."

"Fuck off," I say but nudge him playfully.

To be honest, I hadn't given the other items on her list any more thought, but at the mention of it, I move to Gabby and pull her to me so we're dancing together. Well, she dances, and I just sort of exist in front of her. "What item are we crossing off the list tonight?"

I panic when her eyes widen. Shit, she probably thinks I'm angling for sex. I should have phrased that differently. Although, now that I've thought of sex, there's no erasing it from my mind.

"What about dance-off or food fight?" I offer coming up with the most PG items I can off the top of my head.

"Those aren't on my list."

"Maybe they're on mine," I say and do some sort of ridiculous dance move that I've seen Joel do when he's drunk and looking for attention. Suffice to say I've seen it a lot.

Soon we're trading bad dance moves and I'm grinning like an idiot. So is she. We've garnered a crowd who cheers for us both, but they're definitely more on her side, so I toss in the towel and bow down to her, giving her the win.

"Come on, dancing queen, I need a drink after that."

She places her hand in mine and I weave through the crowd to the bar where I order us both water.

"Killer dance moves, my man," the bartender says, winks, and puts two shots in front of us with the water. "On the house."

I give him my thanks as Gabby laughs beside me.

"What are you laughing at?"

"You," she says. "I'm pretty sure that bartender was hitting on you and you didn't even realize it."

"He was?"

She nods several times. "I've been up to this bar a dozen times tonight and he hasn't so much as glanced my way. Then you show up and he's offering free drinks and winks to go."

"Must be my dance moves."

She laughs softly. "Must be."

We take the shot and drink our water as we catch our breath and crowd watch. People just keep piling into the place, making it feel a little claustrophobic. Gabby's head starts to pop up, standing on her tiptoes to see over the crowd in different directions.

"Who are you looking for?"

"No one. I was trying to see if there was a restroom up here."

My height makes it easy to see over the crowd. I nod to the back right corner. "Come on. I'll clear the way."

Even for me, it's a tough push. Large groups are trying not to lose one another by holding hands, creating a fence of people. I can feel Gabby sticking close, a hand at my back. At five paces away, she lurches forward and her hands grapple at my side as she tries to keep herself upright. I turn in time to see the two guys, more drunk and obnoxious than the rest, that bumped into her.

"Watch where you're going." I growl as I bend down to help Gabby get to her feet. She rubs at her elbow, which must have taken the brunt of her fall.

One of the assholes looks slightly remorseful as he offers his help, but when his gaze sweeps Gabby's body and then stops on the left side of her face, he snickers and mumbles, "Butterface."

Gabby tenses under my hold and immediately ducks her head, embarrassment clouding her features.

I've never understood the expression, seeing red, until now. "What the hell did you say?"

He turns away and I want to follow him and punch him so hard and so many times he rues the day he learned such a dick word, but Gabby is shuffling as quickly as she can in the opposite direction, squeezing her little body between cracks in the crowd that only her tiny form could fit through. I shove people out of my way until I reach her.

"Hey, wait." I wrap a hand around her wrist, and she turns to me, tears in her eyes. I pull her the rest of the way until she's leaning against the back wall outside of the restrooms, shielding her from seeing or hearing anything but me.

"That guy's an idiot." I wipe a tear with my thumb. Her lip quivers and she refuses to meet my gaze, so I tip her chin up with a hand. When her greenish-blue eyes finally look into mine like she's waiting for me to erase the bad by saying all the things she wants to believe about herself instead, my chest gets tight. "Beautiful," I croon out the word, not sounding the least like Pharrell.

Her lips tip up though encouraging me to continue the verse. I'm trying to hear the rest of the song in my head to remember what comes next when her hands come up to rest on my chest and she pushes onto her tiptoes, pressing her lips to my cheek. It's soft and unsure. Sweet and surprising and all the things inherently good about Gabby.

When she pulls back, my lips tingle with need to reciprocate, to show her exactly how beautiful I think she is. Instead, I nod to the ladies' room. "I'll wait here and then we can get back out there and show off our killer dance moves again."

She smiles, though it's small and doesn't reach her eyes and a fresh desire to hunt down the asshole that made her upset makes me ball my hands into fists. "I just want to go home."

nineteen

Gabby

*S*unday evening, Blair is still hanging around my apartment. After we left the club last night, she took one look at me and demanded answers. She hasn't left my side since. She even slept in my room at the cabin, leaving Wes sad-faced and completely cock blocked.

"I'm fine. Seriously. Go study. I know you have a test tomorrow."

She still doesn't budge.

Making an X over my heart, I say, "Cross my heart. I'm really okay. It happened. It's happened before. It's probably going to happen again. I'm okay."

"Why don't you come with me to The White House? The guys usually have movie nights on Sunday, so you can hang with them while Wes and I study."

"And make out."

"I don't have time for making out. Well, not much time. Come on." She sticks out her bottom lip in a pout.

"Fine, fine. It beats sitting here by myself. Can you bring me back after or are you staying at Wes' tonight?"

"Probably staying, but I can drop you off later."

The White House is the quietest I've ever heard it. Wes is waiting in the TV room with bags of takeout, books spread out on chairs and he's wearing the reading glasses I know Blair likes so much. The way her eyes light up at seeing her boyfriend… yep, no way I'm going in there.

"Where is everyone? I thought it was movie night."

"Joel is at Katrina's house and I think Nathan went to the dorms. Zeke's upstairs."

"Then that's where I'll be," I say to the room. Wes and Blair either don't hear me or just don't answer.

On the way up the stairs to the second level, I can hear a basketball bouncing off the gym floor.

The door closes loudly behind me and Zeke looks up to see who has intruded on his space. "Back at it, I see."

"Hey. What are you doing here?" His smile stretches wide and some of the nerves I had about seeing him fall away.

"I came with Blair. She and Wes are studying downstairs." I take a seat on the sidelines, prop my back up against the wall, and pull out my craft thread to make a new bracelet. "Don't worry, I'm not going to bother you. I just didn't want to be the third wheel."

He dribbles the ball over to me and I get a good look at him shirtless and glistening with sweat. The ball in his giant hands eases his features and relaxes his shoulders. I've seen it before, but it still amazes me the way he physically changes when he's holding a basketball. He looks younger and happier. Dare I say carefree even.

"On second thought." I push to my feet. "Can you help me dunk? I've always wanted to, but you know." I motion in front of all five foot four inches of me.

A playful smirk tips up one side of his mouth. "Yeah, alright." He squats down and motions for me to move behind him. "Grab my shoulders and use my leg as a step."

I do as instructed, and he links his arm around my leg balancing me as I lift the other one up and then miraculously I'm on his shoulders. "Woah, don't drop me, it's a long way down. When you fall, does your body hit the ground at triple speed because of the distance?"

He chuckles and passes the basketball up to me. We move under the basket. Well, technically I'm eye level with it. "Bend down a little. I want to dunk it not drop it through the net."

I feel his head shake side to side, but he bends down a couple inches.

"Any advice?" I roll the weight of the ball from one palm to the other.

"Don't miss."

I roll my eyes, lift the ball above the rim and bring it down through the net, grabbing on to the rim for good measure.

"Nice," Zeke says, and he moves to rebound the ball and hands it back to me. "Now this time, do it like you mean it."

I get three or four dunks in, gaining a little more confidence each time, before Zeke lifts me off his shoulders. "My turn."

The Tip-Off

I've seen Zeke dunk before, but the tease in his eye and the cocky way he moves as he performs dunks that are more show than practical, is a new brand of hot I didn't realize I was into.

When he finishes showing off, he's out of breath but smiling bigger than I've ever seen and I don't even care that the smile may be due to some sort of hard wood and leather basketball combination high, I'm just glad to witness it.

"How ya doing? I didn't get a chance to see you before we left this morning." Zeke and I were in separate cars coming back from the lake. A day without seeing him has not made me feel any less humiliated that he was there to witness such an awful incident.

"Good."

His stare tells me he was looking for more than a pacifying answer.

"I'm good," I say again, but I smile reassuringly this time. "Thank you, again, for last night."

"Nothing to thank me for. I'm glad I was there. I'm gonna grab a quick shower and watch a movie or something if you wanna join."

"Can I pick the movie?"

He raises one eyebrow. "No Nicholas Sparks anything."

He hesitates like he's trying to think of more items to add to the 'will not watch list' but doesn't come up with anything before I say, "Deal."

Sitting on Zeke's bed, I scan through the options while he showers. My phone pings with a text.

Mom: How are you? Just checking in. We

haven't heard from you in a week. Call soon. Love, Mom.

I snicker at the way she signs her text.

Me: Things are great. Don't worry. I'll call tomorrow. Xo

Bless her heart, I know my mother is trying to give me space now that I'm living on my own, but when I go a few days without calling, she imagines the worst. I'm sympathetic to her need to know I'm safe, but if I checked in as often as she wanted me to it'd be too much like I was still living at home.

Zeke reappears smelling divine like soap and just… Zeke. He's left his shirt off and only wears a pair of grey sweatpants that sit low on his hips.

He runs a hand over his head. "What did you find?"

I'm silent too long, staring at the wall of muscle greedily when he calls my name.

"Yeah, sorry, I got distracted texting my mom."

He sits on the edge of the bed and I scoot over to make more room for him. We settle on a movie and then stretch out next to each other to watch.

We're only a few minutes in before the tension in the room makes me start to ramble. "Is watch a movie still code for make out or have I been out of the game too long?"

He answers with a chuckle. "What?"

"I'm just curious if you asked me up here to make out or if we're really watching this movie."

The Tip-Off

He just shakes his head. "Watch the movie, beautiful."

twenty

Zeke

The next day I'm in the weight room when Wes tracks me down.

"There you are. I've been looking everywhere for you."

I pull my headphones down around my neck but go right into my next set of squats. "Been right here," I grunt out.

He waits until I've finished and moved to add more weight before he asks, "Everything okay?"

My eyes narrow and concern flashes in his. "Everything's fine. Why?"

Immediately, I regret giving him more ground because the concern turns to amusement. "Maybe because this is your third workout today. Is this the workout of a man with a mission or a man that is working off his sexual frustration?"

I flip him off, but he's not totally off base. "Just focused. I've got interviews coming up, graduation, I got my invitation to the combine... my head is spinning."

I'm feeling... anxious and all sorts of unprepared and no amount of working out seems to help.

He moves to help me add on the appropriate weight to the other side of the bar and asks, "So the crazy amount of working out isn't because you're in a Gabby-induced blue ball hell?"

"No."

Wes stills with the weights, waiting for me to say more.

"We're just..." Friends seems like the wrong word, but it's the only one I can think of. "We're friends is all."

"Alright, if you say so."

I do another set with him spotting me. When I rack the weight, he helps me unload the bar wordlessly. He sits on a bench and looks around the room. "I can't believe this is all really happening. It's not going to be the same next year without you. We had a lot of good times. I'm gonna miss it."

"Me too." I will. It's been the best four years of my life, but it's the next years of my life that I've been working toward for as long as I can remember.

"Does Sara still think you'll go top five?"

"Depends on which team gets the top picks. Suns could be a possibility. They've had a crap season and Sara says there's been some interest there, but everything is up in the air." I shrug. "I'm just gonna show up and hope I get picked up by someone who will give me some floor time next year."

I drain my water bottle and we sit, contemplative and nostalgic. Finally, Wes stands. "You done for the night?"

"Yeah, I was about to head out."

"Good. We're going to The Hideout." He holds up a hand before I can protest. "Joel insisted that we need to officially celebrate my getting the coaching job and if I have to go, so do you."

"How many more last hurrah parties you think he's going to throw?"

Wes chuckles. "My guess? A lot."

It's just the roommates tonight. Which is nice. Since Wes and Joel got girlfriends, we don't hang like this much anymore. I'm like ninety-nine percent sure their girlfriends are going to drop in "unexpectedly" later, though.

When we got to The Hideout, it was some relief to find out that Gabby was working and I wouldn't have to watch the door wondering if she was going to show up with Blair and Katrina. But just being in the same room has me a little on edge. When she's close, I start to forget my reasons for not making a move on her. When she's bringing me food, it's especially hard.

Appetizers and entrees are piled in front of us. Joel ordered damn near one of everything on the menu, most of which is strictly off-limits until I drop another two pounds. I stick to water and salad, which makes the guys snicker. Whatever, they can laugh all they want, but I know they'd do exactly the same thing if they were in my shoes.

"I grabbed this in case you were still hungry." Gabby sets a bowl of steamed vegetables in front of me and my mouth waters.

"You're an angel."

"And what better to chase carrots than Jager." Joel passes out shots and then raises his in the air and looks at Wes. Wes and Nathan raise their shots. It's not like I can say no when it's in honor of Wes' job, so I lift mine too. "To Coach Dubya."

It's the first of many shots, and as it turns out, Blair and Katrina don't show up but I kind of wish they had when the guys are all sloppy drunk and it's just me with enough wherewithal to get us home.

"Hey, Gabby. What time do you get off?"

"Ten minutes."

"Think you could drive us back to the house? We forgot to make sure we had a sober driver. I could call one of the guys, but since you're here."

"Oh, um, I don't have a car here."

I frown. "Okay, well, you can drive mine. That's no problem."

She shifts uncomfortably, eyes on her shoes.

"Gabby?"

"I don't drive."

"What do you mean you don't drive? How do you get around?"

"Blair, Uber, walk." Her cheeks pink. "I could call Blair. She was trying to stay away so you guys could have a proper guys' night, but I'm pretty sure she's waiting by the phone for Wes to call so she can run over and see him."

I glance back at Wes. His eyes are half-closed. "Don't think he's gonna be awake that long. Wait, how are you going to get home?"

She flushes again. "Uber."

Brady calls for her and she offers a meek wave as she walks away. I text Mario for backup and round up the guys.

"Alright, buddy, time to get out of here," I say to Wes and help him to his feet.

"Blair here?"

"Nope, just us guys."

"Fuck, I miss her. Is that weird?" he asks, words slurred. "I don't care. I love that girl."

I say nothing, just hold him steady as we move to the door. I'm about to write off his sentiments as drunken babble when he looks me dead in the eye and says, "Don't be such a hard ass all the time. You're focused, I dig it, and you're about to get everything you ever wanted, but it won't be enough if you're all alone. Ball won't be enough."

Gabby

I hide in the back until Mario shows up to drive the

guys home. Every humiliating moment of the past two weeks and Zeke has to be present for all of them. Why couldn't I just lie and tell him my license was expired or something not as embarrassing as the fact I haven't been able to get back behind the wheel since my car accident?

I see Zeke look around for me, but eventually he ducks out too and I slump against the counter and breathe a sigh of relief. I'm already off the clock, so I grab my stuff and head out to wait for my Uber.

When I push out the front door, Zeke steps away from the building.

"What are you doing here? I thought you guys left."

"They did," he says. "I wanted to make sure you got home okay."

"That's really not necessary."

"Actually, it is. I don't have a ride now either."

It's a short drive, less than five minutes this late at night, and when the car pulls up in front of my place, I give my thanks to both men.

"Give me a minute," Zeke tells the driver and follows me up the sidewalk and to my front door.

"Do you want to come in for a drink or we could watch a movie or something?"

"I should get back, check on the guys. In the future, if you need a ride, then call me."

"Yeah, okay." I roll my eyes. Of all the people I might call for a ride, he's not even in the top ten. How mortifying.

"I'm serious."

"Oh, I know, but it's no big deal. I've got it covered just fine. I can take care of myself."

He lifts a brow.

"Goodnight, Zeke."

The next night I'm finishing up the assigned reading for my economics class when I get a text. I smile like a fool when I see Zeke's name.

Zeke: You home?

Me: Yep

Zeke: I'm in the parking lot.

I'm still staring down at the phone when another comes in.

Zeke: Bring your purse and lock your door, you're coming with me.

twenty-one

Gabby

Zeke leans on the hood of his black 4-Runner, one long leg crossed over the other.

"Hey," I call a little tentatively and a whole lot breathless. "What are we doing?"

He holds up the keys and jingles them in the air. "We're gonna sit in my car."

"Ooookay." I head to the passenger side.

"Uh-uh, that's my side." He steps in front of me, his big frame blocking my way.

"I don't drive."

"Who said anything about driving?" I still don't budge until he adds, "I made a playlist special for the occasion."

Zeke opens the door for me, and I slide into his seat with a nervous laugh because it's so far back I can't even see over the steering wheel. I adjust the seat as Zeke runs around and climbs into the passenger side.

His car is clean, and his scent permeates the air. He reaches over and turns the car on and then settles back into the leather seat, hooking his phone up and finally smiling as Billy Ocean's "Get Outta My Dreams, Get Into My Car" starts playing. Then he reaches into the back seat and brings back a plastic bag which he sets on his lap and starts to dig through with excitement.

"Water." He hands me a bottle. "And one for me." He puts his water between his legs and continues to rummage. "And you get your choice of... well, everything." He dumps the contents out into his lap. Chips, candy, gum.

"You're not going to try and kiss me, are you?" I ask playfully. His eyes widen in surprise or maybe panic, and I laugh. "Just checking before I eat an entire bag of Funyuns."

He hands them over with a grin. "You're safe."

I dig into the onion-flavored rings and Zeke shuffles through the playlist, grinning adorably each time I laugh or smile at the songs he selected.

I'm enjoying his company and have completely forgotten the reason behind this charade until he asks, "Have you driven since the accident?" There's no judgment in his tone, but I feel inferior in front of this man who, as far as I can tell, isn't scared of anything except hashtags.

"No." I stare at the last Funyun in my bag.

He ducks his head down so his face is in front of mine. "Hey, I get it. It's gotta be scary to get back behind the wheel after something like that."

A full-body tremor takes over at the memory. The out of control feeling as the car had hydroplaned and then the moment just before impact when I had been helpless to do anything but brace myself for the worst.

"I used to love to drive," I say and run a hesitant hand over the steering wheel. "I had a cherry red convertible. Blair was so jealous because her parents got her this used beater with the manual locks and windows, but my dad works at a car dealership, so I got the whole new car with a bow on top for my sweet sixteen." I sigh at the memory. "We looked good riding around in that car, blasting Beyoncé."

"I bet you did."

"When my parents wanted to replace my car with the insurance money, I wouldn't let them get another nice car. I made them get me an awful little used, compact number." I point to it in the parking lot. "I thought maybe it'd help, but I haven't been able to drive it either."

"I've got an idea," he says and puts on his seat belt. "Drive my car over and park next to yours."

"Zeke, I—"

"Buckle up, buttercup."

I do as he says, but I don't move to put the car into drive. "I can't."

"Sure, you can. I'm right here. I won't let anything happen to you." Then he pats the dash of his car. "Or you, sweetheart."

To be honest, I'm not sure why I put the car in drive, but I do, and it gives me a rush.

"Good girl. Now just pull beside your car. It looks so lonely over there by itself."

I let the car roll forward just an inch, my breath hitches, I slam my eyes closed and hit the brakes. Hard.

To his credit, Zeke says nothing for several long moments until I pry my eyes open.

"You good?"

I laugh at the absurdity of the question. "No."

He chuckles quietly. "You're doing great. Take your time."

Sweat beads up at the nape of my neck, but finally, I pull the car out of the parking spot and drive it the short distance. I leave so much space between my car and his, I'm taking up two spots, but I did it! I let go of the steering wheel and turn to Zeke, who smiles like a fool. He puts the car in park, and I unbuckle and throw myself at him. Arms around his neck, I have him in a death grip. "Thank you."

One arm caresses my back. "I didn't do anything."

I pull back so I can look him in the eye. "I just drove."

"I know. I was there. It was all you."

Brown eyes sparkle at me. My chest is heaving, and I feel so alive and happy. Our mouths are so close. My gaze darts to his lips. Funyuns, be damned, I want to kiss him.

"The only thing that would make this better is if we climbed into the back seat and made out." I waggle my brows at him.

His breaths are coming as fast and labored as mine, but he chuckles and lifts me from where I'm perched awkwardly on the middle console, back into the driver's seat.

"It's the Funyuns, isn't it?"

The Tip-Off

"No, beautiful girl, it's not the Funyuns. I want to take you somewhere."

twenty-two

Zeke

Fraternity parties are not my scene, but the look on Gabby's face when I pull up to frat row is worth it. The front lawn of Sig Nu is filled with people holding cups and I can hear the bass of the music inside as we walk up.

"Attend a frat party is on my list," she says excitedly, her eyes taking it all in.

"Is it?" I ask like I don't have the damn list memorized.

She hangs tight as we enter through the ornate wooden doors, columns on either side, and the Greek letters displayed proudly. From the outside, it's all old money and prestige, but inside it's just like any other college party. The music is loud, and people are everywhere.

"Z? What are you doing here, man?" Malone catches us just inside. He's a member of this fraternity so on the rare occasions I have stumbled into a party on frat row, it's been this one.

"Heard there was a party."

"You heard right. Maxwell got a job on Wall Street." He leans toward Gabby. "Daddy pulled some strings, but you didn't hear it from me."

"Nathan around?" I ask.

"Haven't seen or heard from him today, but I'm sure he'll show up. I gotta make a liquor run. Keg's in the kitchen."

"Shall we?" I ask when he's gone.

Gabby nods, wearing her excitement all over her pretty face. She pulls me to the kitchen, so much pep in her step she's practically floating.

"Do you want a beer?" I pull a cup from the counter and hold it up. When she signals yes, I fill it and place it in her eager hand.

"You're not drinking?"

"Nope. I'm flying out tomorrow morning to interview with Orlando, so tonight I'm on list duty." I hold out my arm and she loops hers through it. "We've crossed off frat party, I'm positive someone has a beer bong around here, and if there are no fights by midnight, I'll push Malone into the drunkest group of guys I can find."

She drinks the first beer like it's her job to get drunk as fast as possible. When Nathan finally shows up, it becomes Mission Sober Impossible. I hang back and let them have their fun, holding the beer bong when appropriate, and doing my best to make sure Gabby doesn't drink so much that I'm going to have to hold her hair back.

As it is, I'm not sure I feel comfortable taking her back to her place alone, which is a real problem for me since I can't seem to stop imagining her body underneath mine, fisting my hands in all that blonde hair, and devouring that sweet mouth. But it's not just about the physical. If it were, I wouldn't be so conflicted.

I've given up trying to deny there is something between us. Despite my trepidations, I want to spend time with her. That doesn't change the fact that I'm leaving in a few weeks. And Gabby is, for all her attempts to convince the world otherwise, naïve and inexperienced. She's not the kind of girl you sleep with one week and then run off and forget the next.

"We should go skinny dipping again," Gabby says too loudly. The guys around us snicker and one pipes up, "Hell yeah!"

Nathan looks uncomfortable for the first time and I feel for the guy. Drunk Gabby has no filter and he's probably imagining her naked. Shit, now I'm uncomfortable because I don't like the idea of him picturing her that way, and also now *I'm* thinking about her naked again.

"Maybe we should get you home."

"No way. It's an unspoken rule of the list that you can't leave a frat party before it's over."

"I'm not sure these things ever really end. Eventually, people just pass out on the lawn."

Her eyes go wide. "See, we don't want to miss that!"

Nathan comes to the rescue. He drapes an arm

around her shoulder and says, "He's right. It's all downhill from here. Let's go back to the house and chill."

When she finally agrees, my shoulders sag with relief that I'm not gonna have to pull an all-nighter. Showing up tired to meet the coach of the Magic wouldn't look great. When she passes out as soon as we get her into my car, though, it's obvious she wasn't going to make it much longer. I drive us back to the house and get Gabby tucked into my bed. I head downstairs wondering in what universe I'm sleeping on the couch the night before the biggest interview of my life.

I'm tossing and turning, trying to get comfortable when the creak of the floor catches my attention. It could be any number of people, three roommates, two with girlfriends, but the way my body reacts — hyperaware - and this tight feeling in my chest, I know it's Gabby even before she whispers my name.

"I'm right here." I sit up. "Are you okay?"

"No."

She comes into view, tan legs bare. She's wearing one of my t-shirts, but it's so big on her it fits more like a dress. A short dress that looks too good to be real.

"What's wrong?" I'm almost to my feet when the ghost of a smile plays on her lips.

"I don't want to sleep alone."

"You're drunk."

"Drunk Gabby wants the same things as Sober Gabby."

"The fact that you're talking about yourself in the third person makes me seriously doubt the validity of that statement."

"Interesting. Take off your pants and let's talk about it in more detail."

I chuckle, God help me. "Not happening."

"Will you at least come sleep in your bed? I know you have an early flight and the meeting tomorrow." She motions to the couch. "Sleeping down here can't be comfortable."

"I'll survive."

"You are so stubborn." She lifts the hem of her shirt.

"What are you doing?"

"If you won't sleep upstairs, then I'm going to take off my clothes and join you on the couch."

I reach her just as she gets the shirt high enough to reveal the pink lacy underwear underneath. Never gonna be able to un-see that. "Stop. Okay, you win." I turn her so she's facing the way she came. "Keep your clothes on. I'm right behind you."

And that's how I end up sleeping in the same bed as Gabby for the first time. And as for sleep – I would have fared better on the couch. You can't lie next to a hot chick and not think about sex, and you can't sleep with a boner. You just can't. It's science.

twenty-three

Gabby

"I heard you did the walk of shame this morning."

Blair sets her backpack down in the chair across from me and takes the seat beside it.

"Walk of awesome," I say without looking up from my laptop. "Joel was right about that."

"So…?" The tone of her voice begs for details and I look up.

"Nothing happened. Just sleep. If my memory is correct. I might have tried to take my clothes off, but he stopped me."

"The man has willpower." She lifts her chin and looks to my laptop. "Whatcha doing?"

I spin it around so she can see the screen.

"I don't get it."

"It's a playlist for Zeke. All songs that mention the

NBA in the lyrics. Plus, a couple songs by Shaq because who doesn't love an NBA star trying to rap?"

She raises both eyebrows and snorts. "If you say so."

I add one last song to the list and then shoot a text to Zeke with the link. "Done."

"Good. Are you ready to register for classes next semester?" She lets out a little squeal. "I can't believe we're finally going to take classes together. I was thinking we should take Ethics on Monday, Wednesday, Friday, and then on Tuesday and Thursday Business Marketing. Those two are prerequisites for the MBA program."

"Actually, I'm not sure."

"About which one?"

"Either."

She frowns. "What do you mean?"

"It's just, I need to check with my advisor first. I'm not sure about a couple of my online class transfers."

"Okay. Well, when are you meeting with her?" I bite my lip and my best friend sees right through me. "Gabs, all the good classes will fill up. You need to talk to her as soon as possible."

"I'll stop by today."

She keeps staring at me until I give in. "Fine, I'll go now."

She claps her hands. "This is going to be so exciting!"

Blair walks with me to Stanley Hall. "Call me after and let me know. Do you work tonight?"

"No. I'm off."

"I could come over tonight around eight and we could select classes while watching *The Bachelorette*." She's staring at her phone, probably her schedule, as she attempts to make plans and I'm thankful because I feel guilt rising as I blow her off.

"Raincheck? I need to catch up on reading and sleep tonight."

"Tomorrow? I've got a few hours during lunch."

"I'm working the afternoon shift, but we'll figure it out." I hug her quickly. "I'll call you later."

I make my way up to the third floor of Stanley Hall. Dr. Rainey is in her office and I knock on the open door to get her attention.

"Gabby." She pulls her red-rimmed glasses from her face and smiles. "Come in."

"Do you have a few minutes? I was wondering if I could talk to you about classes next semester?"

"Of course, have a seat." She puts the glasses back on and her fingers fly over the keyboard. "Let me just pull up your transcripts."

I twist my hands nervously in my lap as she does. Dr. Rainey is my hero. She built and sold a successful startup all before she was thirty. I have no idea why she's teaching at Valley, but the university is all the better for it.

"Alright. With this semester's classes, you only need six more credits toward your business degree, and you've satisfied all the core requirements except business law. You're ahead of schedule." She smiles brightly. The benefits of hiding away for three years – I'm ahead of schedule in college course requirements. Two more classes and I'll have my business degree.

"Are you still planning to apply to the MBA program in the fall?"

"I'm not sure," I answer honestly. "I've been looking

into some other programs as well."

"It's good to consider all your options. Valley has a wide range of graduate-level courses and programs. Is there someone I can get in touch with for you? What programs are you considering?"

"All of them."

Her fingers lift from the keyboard and she sits back in her chair. "All of them?"

"I want to explore a bit more before I lock myself into anything. I had my sights set on business before I took my first class and never really entertained anything else."

I don't expect the smile she gives me. "I think that's a really smart idea."

"You do?"

"Yes." She laughs softly. "Take it from someone who switched careers after hating her first job out of college, it's easier and less stressful if you figure out what you want to do before you leave here. Have you talked to anyone in the career resource center?"

"No, not yet." My stomach turns.

"I'd start there. I've heard great things about the new student advisor in the tutor center. I have her name here somewhere." Dr. Rainey flips through some papers on her desk. "Ah, here it is. Her name is—"

"Blair Olson," we say at the same time.

"You know her?"

"Yeah, I do."

"Great. I'd start there."

"Thank you, Dr. Rainey."

She nods. "My pleasure, Gabby. Whatever you decide, I know you're going to do great things."

The Tip-Off

I decide to walk back to my apartment to give myself time to think. At least I'd answered one question today – there's no way to avoid Blair while I try and figure out what the right career path is for me.

It's only about a half-mile from campus, but I move slowly so it takes far longer than it should. I wonder how Zeke's interview went. What exactly do they do at an NBA interview? Ask him to define ball terms? Test his sports history knowledge? He mentioned he'd also get a chance to scrimmage with the team which sounds pretty awesome. I can just picture Zeke playing with all those big, strong NBA players. It's where he belongs.

I'm still not sure where I belong after Valley. I thought it was being with Blair, starting our own company, and being lady bosses, but the older I get, the more I realize that I wasn't meant to run a company. Not like Blair. Her passion and excitement for business is obvious and she's going to be an amazing CEO someday, but I want simpler things. I want to do work that feeds my soul and I want to spend my days remembering that I lived for a reason. I want to say yes to all that life has to offer, not be stuck inside an office working insane hours. Life's too short.

Well past eight o'clock, Zeke finally responds to my text about the playlist.

Zeke: This list is awesome.

Me: I know, right? How was the interview? Also, in what year did the Chicago Bulls win seventy-two games?

I'm holding the phone waiting for his response when it rings instead.

"Hi."

"Hey. I'm too tired to text." Zeke's deep voice makes me smile, and even over the phone, I can hear the exhaustion. "What are you up to?"

"Watching *The Bachelorette* and looking up basketball trivia."

"Ninety-five-ninety-six season," he responds and then yawns.

"What?"

"You asked what year the Bulls won seventy-two games."

"Oh, right."

"Why are you looking up basketball trivia? I didn't know you even liked basketball."

"I like basketball as much as any sport. Which isn't all that much admittedly. I was thinking about your interview and then I started to wonder what types of questions they'd ask, and the next thing I knew I was watching YouTube videos of NBA records."

"That was a great team. Jordan, Pippen, Rodman, Longley, Kukoc."

"Is it weird to think someday people are going to be talking about you that way?"

"Honestly? No. It's the dream. It's what I've worked toward my whole life. I've done everything I can to get myself ready for this next step, but I'll have to keep on proving myself for a long time before people lump me in with guys like that."

"They will, though."

"God willing." He yawns and I know I should let him

go so he can sleep, but I missed him today, weird as that sounds.

"So today went well?"

"Yeah, it went well. The facilities are insane, coaches are great. It's a waiting game for now until the draft lottery to see how things shake out. I'm going to Phoenix next week to meet with the Suns."

"Suns would be cool. I bet the guys would love having you close so they could come watch games and stuff."

"You wouldn't think it was cool?"

"Sure."

He laughs. "Thought you'd be more pumped at the idea you'd be close enough to rope me into more shenanigans."

"You underestimate my abilities. I can find a way to do that no matter how far away you are."

"I have no doubt." I know he's smiling as he says it and I feel a little pang of sadness that he's going to leave in a few weeks and I probably won't see him again. He'll be in the NBA and I'll be just a normal college kid trying to find my way. "Speaking of shenanigans, I was wondering if you're free Thursday?"

"I work during the day. What's up?"

He clears his throat. "Every year the Valley athletic department does an award ceremony for student-athletes. It's a bit stuffy, suit and tie and the awards themselves last a few hours and can get pretty boring..."

"Wow, you're really selling this."

"*But* there's free food and booze and everyone will be there. Wes is bringing Blair, Mario and Vanessa, Joel and Katrina. Do you want to be my date?"

My stomach does a happy flip. "Sounds fun. I'm in."

"Cool. It starts at seven. Wes and I have to be there a little early to help with some setup stuff, but it shouldn't take too long. Pick you up at six?"

"It's a date," I sing-song.

"Yep, it's a date."

twenty-four

Gabby

Thursday night finds me in my room trying on every
dress I own. Blair assured me that any dress would do,
that the only people who get super dressed up are the
athletes that are accepting or handing out awards, but
I'm not dressing for the student-athletes of Valley, I'm
dressing for Zeke.

At five minutes until six, I go back to the first dress I
tried on, a deep red one-shoulder gown that's long and
hugs my body from top to bottom. It's classy because it
covers so much skin, but sexy because of the way it
accentuates my curves. I opt for black heeled sandals
and leave my hair down and in its usual big wave style
that hides the left side of my face. I keep my makeup
simple and skip the jewelry. I'm hoping for *holy shit*, but
in a *she doesn't even look like she tried* sort of way. Or in

Zeke's case, I'm going for *let's bang right fucking meow.*

At the top of the hour, he knocks. Right on time.

"It's open," I call and shove all my necessities from my purse into a little handbag for the night.

I look up when I hear the door open and prepare to tell him I just need two minutes, but the sight of Zeke takes my breath away.

"Wow, Gabby, you look... wow."

"Right back at you." I abandon my purse and walk toward him. He's wearing the hell out of a black tuxedo, complete with a bow tie. I do a circle around him, taking in every inch. Good God. "In fact. I think we should just skip this award thingy."

"Wes and Blair are waiting in the car."

"Damn them," I tease as I cross the room to get my clutch.

On our way out the door, he places a hand at my back. The touch sends goosebumps racing over my skin and I inhale sharply. He must hear my reaction because he mutters an apology and moves his hand.

The awards are held inside the field house. A platform covers one side of the gym floor, chairs set up in tidy rows facing it. Zeke and Wes lead us to the opposite side, where a bar and cocktail tables are set up. We're among the first people here, but even so, the eye candy is incredible.

"It's like Vanity Fair meets Sports Illustrated up in here." I unapologetically gawk at a tall, blonde girl with tan skin and an athletic build. I'm guessing tennis or maybe volleyball.

"Back in a bit," Wes says and drops a kiss to Blair's mouth.

I'm still taking in the number of hot jocks in my proximity that I almost forget Zeke is next to me. Also, I'm a liar.

"Hey." His fingertips graze my elbow and my attention snaps fully to him. "It's assigned seats." He hands over a ticket and I notice Blair holds one too. "I'll be back as soon as I can. Don't have too much fun without me."

We stare at one another, each taking the other in, electricity humming between us until Wes calls after him.

"Back soon," he mutters and follows after Wes.

Blair and I find our seats. A girl in a halter dress with shoulders like a linebacker hands us a program. It's thick, pages and pages of Valley athletes and a schedule for the night. Zeke was right – this thing is going to last a really long time. Fine by me so long as Zeke brings all that tall, dark, sexiness back and sits beside me... or on top of me, pulls me into a corner. My thoughts run away with possibilities.

When the guys return, they bring with them the rest of the team and their dates. Mario and Vanessa are sitting with the baseball team, but V waves and promises to find us after the awards.

A flask is pushed into my hands just as the lights dim. I give Zeke a questioning glance and he looks a little sheepish. "It's tradition."

The liquor, pure vodka, I think, burns as I take a sip. I hand it to Blair and then do my best to pay attention to the stage as every athlete is recognized and the coaches give a nice little speech about how honored they are to work with such talented young people, yadda,

yadda, yadda.

I'm stifling a yawn when Wes and Zeke stand up and leave without a word.

"Where are they going?" I whisper to Blair.

She smiles coyly. "Zeke is getting the Harper Award."

"What is that?"

She points to the stage as Coach Daniels appears for the second time. "The Harper Award is given each year to a Valley University student-athlete who exemplifies leadership and teamwork. It's my pleasure to introduce senior Wes Reynolds to announce this year's recipient."

Blair leans over. "Look how handsome he looks in a suit. I convinced him to buy one to wear at games next year when he's coaching."

I give her a thumbs up and I gotta admit he does fill it out nicely. The field house gets quieter than it's been all night as Wes starts his speech. He tells everyone about how he met Zeke when they played against each other in an AAU game and gets some laughs over the story of how Zeke's team had won and Wes had tried to be the bigger man by congratulating Zeke after the teams had done the usual player handshake, but Zeke had already slipped on his headphones and tuned out the world.

Wes even gets a little choked up when he talks about his injury. Blair's full on crying and Shaw hands her the flask.

"I'm beyond honored to be the one to give him this award. He's been an opponent, a teammate, a roommate, but today I'm honored to call him a friend and brother."

The Tip-Off

Zeke comes from stage left and I'm on my feet with everyone else in our row screaming and clapping as he accepts his award.

"You're on a date with a Valley celebrity." Blair passes me the flask. "How's it feel?"

"Handsome," I say, and she giggles. "I mean, *he's* handsome. I feel… like if he doesn't kiss me soon, I might die."

twenty-five

Zeke

"Why didn't you tell me you were getting the Harder Award?" She hefts the trophy in one hand.

"*Harper* Award."

"Same difference." Gabby places the trophy down on the little table between us. "Seriously. Why didn't you tell me?"

I shrug and lift my drink to my mouth, take a long swallow of the potent liquor before I respond. "It's not a big deal. Besides, would you have known what I was talking about if I'd told you?"

"Point made." She stares at me with a look I can't decipher. "I would have come with you even if you'd been getting an award for worst player of the year, you know that, right?"

"I do know that." I step around the table in two

strides, finally able to focus only on her. Ever since I walked into her apartment, I've been playing out the night in my head like a Choose Your Own Adventure novel. If I touch her hand, will she shiver at my touch? If I kiss her, will I be able to stop? If I don't make a move soon, will my dick actually fall off from the perpetual blue balls?

"You're stunning in that dress. Scratch that, you're stunning. The dress is just along for the ride." The smile she flashes at me is all the recognition and trophy I need tonight.

"You clean up nice yourself. Not too late to consider a change in career." She runs a hand over the lapel of my jacket. "Something that requires you to dress like this more often. Investment banker, attorney, reporter—"

"Male model."

She lifts her hands up to her face and peers at me through a rectangle she makes with her fingers. "Work your angles. Smize. Yeah, like that. Now take it off. Sloowly."

"You're a little too good at that."

"I watched every season of *America's Next Top Model*."

"Never heard of it."

She makes an exaggerated gasp. "Tyra Banks? Nigel Barker? Well, we must rectify this situation. Grab your golden statue, honey, we've got to get home and watch every season naked. Your career depends on it."

"Always trying to get me naked." I chuckle and step closer. "What would you do with me if you did?"

Her blue-green eyes widen, and she watches my fingers with rapt attention as I move them to her cheek and push her hair on the left side of her face back giving me a better view of her.

"Whipped cream bikini, pillow fight, naked wrestling, maybe we could stop by the store and get one of those kiddie pools and fill it with Jell-O."

I open my mouth to speak, close it, open it... I've got nothing.

"You should see your face." She laughs and then fixes her features back into a stoic expression. "But seriously."

"Life with you is never boring, is it?"

She shrugs and a little bit of her mask slips. I'd always thought of Gabby hiding behind her hair to cover her external scars, but maybe her words hide the ones I can't see. "Come on. I want to show you something."

"Your penis? Because if you're not about to get naked, I'm going to be sorely disappointed."

I'm shaking my head as we step away from the party, the voices and the laughter becoming distant noise as we get farther away. Being with Gabby is like wearing my headphones except instead of music drowning out the noise, it's her making everything else fade to the background.

"Where are we going?" she asks as we enter the darkened hallway.

"Almost there." I take her hand as I lead the way, navigating the place like I live here. And basically, I have for the last four years. I give a glance over my shoulder to make sure no one sees us. Last thing I need is someone following along.

Gabby looks intrigued, if not a little skeptical about our location. All else fails, I'll take my dick out and pretend it's the main attraction. It's not. On second thought, Gabby might be more excited about that than what I have planned, but this is important for me. I can't sleep with her, can't treat being with her as if it's all part of a list.

Yeah, I'm leaving, and I think she understands that, but I need to know for sure that if we have sex, she's not going to regret that it was some guy who took off a couple weeks later. You can't un-ring that bell. She treats it as if it's as insignificant as doing a beer bong at a party, but deep down, I know it's important to her.

"Oooh the boy's locker room," she croons as I place a palm on the heavy wooden door and give it a push open.

"Here we go." I flip on the light to my home away from home away from home. The locker room at Valley is well-kept and clean. The lockers are light oak and have double doors. Every player has his own with his name and number displayed on a screen, and in front, a chair for those game-time pep talks. It's nothing like people expect. They're probably thinking something keen to their high school locker rooms with rickety metal lockers and a smell that never seems to go away, but they take care of us here at Valley.

"Wow. This is nice." Gabby turns a circle as she takes in the room. When she sees my name, she walks toward the locker and touches it. My dick twitches, which is weird, right? But I've never brought a girl to see my locker before.

"Back here."

I motion for her to follow me past the lockers to an open area we use to watch game film. I walk around the roadrunner mascot painted on the floor. "Don't step on Ray or it's seven seasons of bad luck."

Propped up against the white screening wall is my number fifty jersey, framed and ready to hang. I stop in front of it.

"Is this your game jersey?"

I nod. "Yeah. They're retiring it."

"Zeke, that's amazing."

"Thanks. Yeah, I think it's pretty awesome that I get to leave a little something behind."

She kneels to look it over for a moment before standing and facing me. "You're leaving behind more than just a jersey."

"Yeah, I know. The team did great things this year and our names will be in the record books forever, but this is all mine."

"I meant friendships, memories. You've made some of those, right?"

"Not as many as I should have probably." It's hard to regret the past four years because of all that I've accomplished, but I'm man enough to admit that I probably could have allowed myself to have a little more fun.

"Not too late," she says and nudges me playfully.

"Isn't it?"

"Every passing minute is another chance—"

"To turn it all around," we finish the *Vanilla Sky* movie quote together.

She walks to me slowly, or maybe time freezes. Blue-green eyes lock on mine and she runs a tentative hand along the front of my jacket. "What do you say, want to make some memories?"

The Tip-Off

And then I kiss her.

twenty-six

Gabby

When the man makes a move, he makes a freaking move. My lips sting under his crushing kiss and my back finds a wall. What wall? No clue and I don't care about anything but his next breath. Mine are all his and I give them freely.

I've never felt more beautiful as he holds my face in his big hands and feasts on my mouth. It's sweet and hard and. It. Is. Everything.

Zeke's broad shoulders flex. Even through the suit jacket, I can feel his muscles doing their thing. And even sexier that that *thing* they're doing is making out with me. Zeke's hands relinquish my face and roam down my sides. His lips release mine and I miss the feel immediately, but when his mouth finds my neck, I forgive the absence.

"You're so beautiful," he murmurs against my skin and the words tickle my sensitive flesh. "So long... I've waited so long to taste you and you're even sweeter than I imagined."

I'm swooning at his feet with every word and every touch.

He pulls back and flashes me a devilish grin at the same time his hands disappear under the skirt of my dress. Strong fingers stroke the outside of my legs and ride up until he finds the band of lace. He loops his thumbs through at my hips and slides my panties down. I step out of them carefully and he pockets the red scrap of material into his suit jacket.

"A memento?" I barely recognize the raspy voice as my own.

"Just clearing a path."

"To my vagina?"

"I aim to please."

"If that were true, you'd already be naked."

He tsks softly, his mouth so close that I can feel the movement of his lips against my collarbone. He presses flush against me, and I lean into his hard body. Grinding his length so close to my throbbing core, he whispers, "We don't have time for the naked version. Someone could walk in."

My legs tremble at the thought of being caught with Zeke in compromising positions. I don't hate the idea.

"If you're teasing me, so help me God—"

My idle threat goes unspoken because Zeke's fingers slide back under my dress and find my center. I laugh out of happiness and surprise and probably delirium. His deep, throaty chuckle follows mine and he stops. A second's hesitation makes me scared he might pull away.

"Don't stop or I'll die of disappointment." Is the most eloquent thing I can think of, but it does the trick and after another short chuckle he continues.

The orgasm that feels like it's been building for weeks is so close I'm embarrassed by how little effort it requires before I'm trembling and moaning. I clamp my mouth shut realizing I'm being louder than one probably should while having sneaky locker room sex.

"Don't get shy on me now," Zeke says. "Let me hear you."

I unlock my jaw but still refrain from making a sound until he rubs my clit at a speed that demands to be celebrated with vocal recognition. He speaks through the kiss. "Nobody here but me, beautiful girl. Be as loud as you want."

With a nod, I ask him to get the fuck back to it – in much nicer words, of course. He hasn't even broken a sweat when I cry out, saying his name, saying mine, there's a good chance I speak tongues as Zeke brings me to the magical land of orgasmic paradise, and I make plans to visit regularly.

He holds me steady until I return to reality and regain basic motor function. He smooths down my dress and takes my hand.

"Ready to re-join the party?"

"Do we have to?"

He doesn't look any more excited about doing so than I am. "Afraid so." He tucks my hair behind my ear and places a chaste kiss on my lips. He squeezes my hand once before he pulls me toward the door, pushes it open, and holds it for me to walk in front of him.

The Tip-Off

It's another three hours before the party is over. Wes and Blair walked home and since Zeke and I both drank more than we should, we take an Uber back to my place.

"Thank you for tonight. I had fun." The end of the date shouldn't feel awkward when we've already kissed and he's had his fingers inside me, but my heart races as he walks me to the door.

"Me too. You make everything a helluva lot more fun."

"Do you want to come in?" I offer. My body is so amped up, begging to be touched by him again.

He shakes his head. "Not tonight." He steps forward and drops a kiss to my lips. "Goodnight, Gabby."

twenty-seven

Zeke

The next few days go something like this: eat tiny portioned meal that tastes like cardboard, finish said meal still hungry, workout, eat another toddler-sized meal, school, eat (yep, you guessed it – miniature meal), workout, eat, eat some more, and somewhere after exhaustion and hunger takes over, I sleep. There's also a lot of texting with Gabby, which is basically the highlight between all the other must-dos in my day.

I'm lying in bed texting her and wondering if I should invite her over or ask her on a real date when Joel stops by my room. He knocks on the open door to get my attention. "We're going out in thirty."

"Pass."

He makes a sound like a buzzer. "Wrong answer. It's the last Monday of the month, last Monday of the month for the entire school year, last chance to get dollar beers at Prickly Pear, last—"

"Alright, alright. I'll go. Just stop saying the word last. I'm not dying."

He smirks and steps away from my room.

Me: Plans tonight? Looks like I'm going to Prickly Pear with the guys.

Gabby: Same! Blair and Vanessa are over and we're getting ready. It's taking a while because I can't seem to find my favorite pair of red panties.

Me: What color is the second-string?

Gabby: Only one way to find out.

Prickly Pear is packed when we arrive, and the girls aren't here yet, so we grab a bucket of beers and then work our way through the chaos to hunt for a table. All that's available is a four-top so we take it and then Joel goes to grab extra chairs.

I shoot a text to Gabby to let her know we're here and have a table. When I look up, Wes is grinning at me all weird like.

"What?" I ask and set my phone on the table in case Gabby responds.

"Nothing." His grin grows larger.

"Spit it out or stop smiling at me like that."

He takes a drink and then leans back, beer bottle resting on his leg. He's drawing out the moment and holding me in suspense for his own satisfaction. "I just think it's fun to see you like this."

"Like what?"

"Hung up on a chick." He motions to my phone. "Texting her." He lifts his head and points toward my leg which is bouncing under the table. "Anxiously waiting to see her. You're so gone for her. How's this going to work when you leave?"

The reminder that whatever this thing between Gabby and me is – it's only temporary - does a funny thing to my insides. I force both feet to stay glued to the floor, take a swig of beer, and shake my head. "It's not like that. Neither of us are looking for anything serious. Gabby just got to Valley – all she wants is to have a good time and get some of that freshman craziness out of her system."

"Let's say I believe that you two aren't totally into each other." He gives me a pointed look. "I don't, by the way, but for argument's sake, I'll pretend that I do. Gabby might be inexperienced, but she's not acting crazy with anyone but you – that's different than the freshman crazy. And you, you've had four years to hang out and hook up, but until Gabby started coming around, you never did. Why now? What's changed?"

I keep my mouth shut because if I start waxing poetic on how Gabby has made me look at life differently and how we're having fun, seizing the day as Gabby would say, instead of dwelling on the expiration date his smile might get so big his head splits apart. Luckily the girls appear, and I don't have to answer.

I stand as Gabby approaches and pull out the chair next to me. "Hey, you made it. Want something to drink?"

The Tip-Off

She takes a seat and there's a nervous vibe bouncing between us which could be entirely my fault. Wes got all in my head. "That'd be great."

The next two hours go by with Joel telling the girls stories of some of our less than finer moments at Prickly Pear, which turns into a stroll down drunken, embarrassing moments lane, and since most of those nights didn't include me making a drunken spectacle, I find myself out of the hot seat and can just sit back and enjoy our time together.

Maybe it's Joel's insistence to make a production out of every last milestone or maybe the end of my college life is making me nostalgic, but either way, I'm not counting down the minutes until I can go home and go to bed.

I sneak a glance at Gabby sitting beside me. She hangs on every word, every story like it's the most fascinating thing she's ever heard. So filled with hope and possibility of all the moments she's missed and, if I've come to know her like I think I do, planning for how she can have all those experiences and more. I have no doubt she will. Girl is gonna leave a mark on Valley with the time she has left. I'm sad I'll miss watching that. Even sad I'll miss being a part of it.

I slide my foot toward and hook it around her leg. At the contact, she doesn't look directly at me, but I see her confirm my movement out of her peripheral. In response, she angles her body a fraction of an inch in my direction. It's the smallest bit of contact, but the adrenaline rush I feel at our connection is big and exciting like those minutes before tip-off when I'm so psyched for a game I feel like anything is possible.

Well before last call, Joel stands. "I'm gonna head out."

It's the first time I've noticed he didn't drink much tonight. He maybe had three beers which is not the Joel Moreno way. He's usually tossing back Jack and chasing it with a twelve pack. Although now that I think of it, he hasn't really been like that since he started dating Katrina. She wasn't able to come out tonight, so I'd bank on him taking it easy so he could show up at her place later.

"You got a ride?"

He nods to our teammate hanging out at the bar. "Malone's gonna drop me at Katrina's. See you guys tomorrow. Glad you came out, Z."

"Me too," I answer honestly.

The girls took off to the bathroom in a group more than five minutes ago and I find myself watching the door just like Mario and Wes. I look away because didn't I just make a point how I wasn't like Wes or the other guys totally hung up on a girl?

Movement catches my eye and my head turns before I can stop myself. Gabby leads the pack, confidence set in her shoulders, head held high and a playful smile dancing on her face. The only visible sign of uncertainty she wears is the way she holds her right hand in a fist tight against her leg as she walks. Instead of taking their seats, Blair and Vanessa hang back and watch as she approaches me.

When she's within an arm's length away, she extends her right hand, still in a fist toward me. Her eyes dart around and then she leans in and whispers, "Black."

My brow arches in question and she pushes her fist

against my hand and opens. My reflexes are shit while I'm trying to figure out what's going on, but the soft material grazes my hand as it falls to the floor. She gasps at the same time I finally catch sight of the black panties now laying on the ground by my feet.

Our awkward interaction has caught the attention of everyone around us. Wes and Mario careen their necks to see what's going on.

"Are those..." Mario starts but then Vanessa punches him in the arm. "Ouch, what? I just—" Vanessa covers his mouth with her hand. Gabby's face turns crimson.

My senses finally return, and I swipe the panties up and wrap my big hand around them so they're no longer visible. The material is still warm from her body heat and with all eyes on me, it takes every ounce of self-control to stand and shove them in my pocket.

"Gentlemen, ladies." I nod in their direction, make the mistake of looking at Wes who has the smuggest look I've ever seen on his face. It says, *I told you so*, in the most obnoxious tone possible.

Gabby is still reeling in her embarrassment, so I step to her, place both hands on her face, and bring my lips to hers. I'm vaguely aware of the guys chuckling behind us, but I don't care. This girl just handed me her panties in the middle of the bar. Yeah, so she fumbled them. Her execution was weak, but the intent more than makes up for it. What could be hotter or more exciting than a chick giving you their panties? I don't know, but if there is something, I'm sure Gabby will be the one to show me.

I'm two seconds from walking out of here with a

boner, so I break the kiss and press my forehead to hers. "Should probably get out of here before I think too hard about the fact you're not wearing underwear right now."

"Can we go to my place? I have a surprise."

My mind reels with possibilities. "Lead the way, beautiful girl."

twenty-eight

Zeke

*W*e take an Uber to Gabby's place. When we get to the front door, she turns to me and says, "Wait here."

"Outside?"

"Two minutes… maybe three." My face must show my confusion because she adds, "It'll be worth it."

"Yeah, okay."

She lets out a squeal, stands on her tiptoes to kiss me on the cheek, and then rushes into the apartment, shutting the door behind her. My back hits the wall and I let out a breath. I'm anxious and nervous and hella curious about what's going on in there. If she's filled a kiddie pool with Jell-O, I may ask her to marry me on the spot.

The time on my phone says it's well past my bedtime, but I feel confident that whatever is about to go down here will be worth it.

The door opens and Gabby's head pokes out. "Ready?" she asks like she's been waiting on me, but my momma didn't raise no fool, so I say, "If you are."

"Close your eyes."

I start to protest, but then think better of it. There's nothing in there I don't want to see, so it's pointless to put up a fight. When my lids are shut, I hear the door creak and then her hand takes mine and pulls.

Without my sight, the first thing I notice is the sound – Color Me Badd is crooning about how they want to sex me up and I laugh. "You made a sex playlist, didn't you?"

"Duh," she says like I should have expected it.

The music is coming from somewhere not in the living room, it's too faint. The second thing is the smell – matches and wax, she's lit candles.

She drops my hand and her voice comes in a whisper. "Open."

The room is lit with more candles than I can count, giving the dark room a soft glow. "Wow, Gabby this is…"

"There's more." She takes my hand again and leads me toward the bedroom. She's still wearing the shorts and tank top she had on at the bar, and I admire the view. It's a good look on her. They're all good looks on her.

The candles continue in her bedroom, scattered on a table by her bed and on top of a dresser on the far wall. The music is louder here too, and I find the source of the sound coming from her open laptop on her desk.

She's set the mood and though I don't need it, I find

it endearing that she went to such lengths. She obviously had a plan for her first time, and I feel completely unworthy showing up with nothing but a condom and a determination to make tonight everything she ever imagined.

I'd be lying if I said I wasn't hoping the night would end with sex, but now that it is… I'm fucking nervous.

Her eyes are wide, tension bouncing off her as she waits for my reaction.

"This is amazing. Highly flammable, but truly amazing. You did all this for me?"

She nods and lets her chin dip. "Listen, I know that what we're doing is just…" She waves a hand in the air like she's searching for the right word. "Casual, but I guess I still want it to be romantic or memorable or whatever. Is that okay?"

I reach her in a single step and wrap my arms around her. "Just because this thing between us is temporary, it doesn't make this, tonight, our time together, any less special. It's more than okay. It's perfect."

twenty-nine

Gabby

*H*is hands slip under my tank top and I still. Forcing myself to breathe, I let his hands wander up my stomach and eventually to cup my breasts through my bra. He moves his hands to my back and feels for the closure.

"Actually, is it okay if I keep this on?" I pull my tank down to cover the exposed patch of stomach.

He transfers his hands to my hips so fast it's like I've slapped him. "Of course."

I realize I've confused him, so I take the initiative and unbutton my shorts and push them down so I'm naked from the waist down. "I still want to have sex, I'm just more comfortable with my shirt on."

He nods ever so slightly. "Are you sure? We can just—"

"Shut up and kiss me."

The Tip-Off

Zeke lies me on the bed and takes my mouth in a kiss that I feel in my toes. I pull at his shirt until he reaches behind with one arm and pulls it over his head. His lips are back sealed to mine in an instant and he deepens the kiss, tasting and teasing me until I'm confident I could orgasm from this alone.

My heart races and emotion clogs my throat as I slide a hand to his jeans and undo the button. With fumbling fingers, I push the zipper down until I can slip my hand inside and underneath his boxers. He lets out a hiss as I wrap my fingers around his length. It pulses in my hand and there's a bead of moisture at the tip.

Eager to see him and to touch him without the barrier of clothing, I help him ease the jeans and boxers down his legs. He tosses them on to the floor and then pulls me so we're lying on our sides facing one another.

"Your body is… wow, Zeke. I want to see you." If tonight is it – if this is the only chance I have with him, I want to memorize every detail.

He grins and rolls onto his back. "As you wish."

I move to my knees and scoot as close as I can. "Wow. I realize I said that already, but seriously. Wow."

He chuckles and places both hands behind his head. "This is good for my ego."

"Enjoy it because I'm not so sure your penisaurus is going to fit inside me."

"Penisaurus?!" His ab muscles contract as he laughs.

"Cocksaurus. Dicksaurus. Nope, penisaurus is the funniest. Oooh, does yours have a name? I always wondered if guys really did that."

"Nah. Mine doesn't anyway, and it's definitely not the type of thing you ask other dudes."

I tap a finger to my chin as I contemplate the perfect name for Zeke's penis. "Ooooh this could be fun."

"Ya know what else would be fun?" He looks down at his erection and then to my naked bottom half.

I'm on my back with him hovering over me before I can answer, and all the butterflies and nerves are back. I've waited twenty-one years for this. I can't believe I ever considered losing my virginity any other way. This is perfect. With someone I trust and like, someone I can be unapologetically myself around, and someone who makes me feel safe. When I jump, he's always there to catch me.

"I'm nervous," I admit.

"Say the word and we stop."

"No way. I want this, and I want it with you." I wrap my arms around his neck and pull his full weight on top of me. He's not light, but the strength and power of his body blankets and surrounds me in the most blissful way. A mixture of urgency and excitement flows through my veins, and I think he feels the same.

I'm absorbing every kiss, every stroke of his tongue and nibble of his teeth when he runs a hand down my body. He shifts his weight so he can reach the center of me. I tense and my knees pull inward in the smallest bit of hesitation that is all my body's doing because I am so ready. I breathe, relax, and lift my hips so he has full access. He takes advantage of the help and strokes my inner thigh and lower belly, moving closer to my throbbing core with every movement.

When his fingers finally brush against my pussy, I bite down on his shoulder playfully to remind him that I'm not made of glass.

"Open wider for me, beautiful."

I do but worry about what he might see or feel. Am I too wet? Not wet enough? Too bare? Not bare enough? Every insecurity I've ever felt is magnified times a thousand until Zeke climbs back on top of me and kisses all thoughts right out of my head.

He rests his forehead against mine. "You'll tell me if it hurts?"

"Sure."

"Gabby." His tone is a warning.

"I will, but only if you promise not to stop. I trust you."

He leans back so he's sitting on his knees and reaches down for his jeans. He retrieves a condom from his wallet and then tosses his wallet back on the floor. I watch in total fascination as he tears open the foil and sheathes himself. He stays on his knees but grabs a pillow and orders me to lift my hips. When I do, he puts it under me so I'm on full display. I don't have time to be self-conscious, though, because he lines himself at my entrance and the first contact of him against my swollen lips takes my breath away.

Instead of pushing in, he rubs himself on me, circling when he gets to my clit, but then sliding down to the slickness that's gathered between my legs. Over and over, slow and deliberate until I'm shaking beneath him.

I'm floating so close to the sun, reaching for it and feeling the heat of it scorching my skin, when he pushes in. It's only an inch, but I gasp at the intrusion. He stills, but I push down on him wanting more. When it hurts, I tell him, but dig my fingernails into his legs to keep him from doing something crazy like stopping. It's a slow and unsteady pace at first while my body tries to accommodate his size. Gradually though, the pain fades and I'm soaring toward the sun again.

I'd kept my eyes closed through the discomfort, afraid he'd see how much it hurt, but now I want to see it all. His brow creased in concentration, the sweat that beads on his chest, the V-cut that points to his dick, and the mesmerizing way our bodies come together. Our eyes lock and I reach out for the sun and erupt into flames.

He follows right behind me, whispering my name as he does.

I watch as the final shudders of his release fade away. Concern flashes in his expression and he moves off me, settling beside me. "Are you okay? Did I hurt you?"

"It was so much better than okay." I roll on my side so I can look at him. "How long do we have to wait before we can do it again?"

He smiles and brings a hand to my shoulder, sliding it down to my elbow and back in a gentle caress. "Let's see how you feel tomorrow and then we'll talk about it. I've heard it sometimes hurts worse the next day. Which way is the bathroom?"

I stick my bottom lip out in a pout. He kisses it before standing next to the bed and removing the condom. "First door on the right."

When he's gone, I close my eyes and melt into the bed completely satiated. I can almost feel his touch still on me... no wait, he *is* touching me. A warm washcloth slides up my calves and to my thighs. I don't think his intentions are to rile me up again, but as he cleans the apex of my thighs, my sex clenches with desire.

"How come you waited?" he asks when he's satisfied with his work and lays back next to me.

"It wasn't intentional, exactly. After the accident, I pushed everyone away. I couldn't stand to look in the mirror so the idea of letting someone close enough to get me naked or the idea someone would even want to, just seemed ridiculous." I pull at my tank top, which has shifted up, and better cover my stomach. "How old were you the first time?"

"Fifteen."

"Did she have a sex playlist?" I ask, feeling irrationally jealous at the idea of him sleeping with someone else.

He chuckles softly and his hands go back to running up and down my arm. "No, definitely not. The only soundtrack we had was the sound of a basketball game in the distance."

I raise a brow. "You had sex at a basketball game?"

"Not *at* the game. In my car just outside."

"Wow. Scandalous."

"Not my finest moment. I was at an AAU tournament and our team was in the finals, but we had a few hours before the last game and this chick just came up to me and…" He looks sheepish. "I was young and dumb."

I'm quiet for too long wondering if we'd be here now if I'd given up my V-card before the accident. I know he's not sleeping with me just because of the list, but is some part of him doing this because he feels sorry for me?

He lifts my chin with a finger. "I'm glad you waited and I'm glad I got to be your first."

Gabby

The next morning, I wake up as Zeke's leaving. He drops a kiss to my forehead, and I pry my eyes open just enough to get a quick glimpse of him. I don't know what time it is, but I know I haven't slept long.

"Don't go," I mumble.

An adorable groan fills my ear and I know he's leaning down close. "I don't wanna, but I have to get to class. I'll call you later." He presses another kiss to my temple, and I fall asleep before the front door shuts.

At a much later and more acceptable hour, I wake for real. I hop into the shower and stand under the spray for a good ten minutes, smiling as I replay last night. I've heard so many horror stories about first times, but last night was more than I ever dreamed.

I have four texts by the time I'm sitting down to a

late breakfast.

Blair: Wes said Zeke didn't come home. DETAILS!

Blair: HELLO??!!

Zeke: Penisaurus? Honestly, it's the only thing I've been able to think about all morning.

Mom: Call me, Gabriella. Love, Mom.

I text Blair back first because I know she'll keep right on texting me until I answer.

Me: Is there such a thing as a de-flowering party? Or do I at least get a pin to commemorate the achievement? Oooh, a secret handshake maybe?

Blair: SQUEEEEEEEEEEEEEEEEEEEEEEEE EEEEEE

Blair: I'm stopping by after work.

Me: Actually, I'm coming to you. Pencil me in for an appointment around noon.

And to Zeke.

Me: I'd say I'm sorry, but I'm not a liar. How is Tony this morning?

Zeke: Tony?

Me: Eh, you're right. It's not a Tony, maybe a Cliff or a Tom.

Zeke: Did you just try and name my dick Cliff?!

Me: He deserves a name. What are you up to tonight?

Zeke: No plans. I leave for Chicago tomorrow and will be gone through the weekend.

Me: Does Cliff have to go?

Zeke: Afraid so. I'm pretty attached to him.

Zeke: Also, hard no to Cliff.

Me: Wanna hang out tonight?

Zeke: Yeah, I'll text you when I'm done with my afternoon workout.

Instead of texting, I call my mom on my way to campus and give her the parent-friendly version of what I've been up to lately.

"I've gotta go, Mom, I'm just getting to campus."

"Be careful and have fun."

"I will, Mooom." I can't help but groan a little at the constant reminder to be careful.

I hang up as I approach the library. Being on campus

still brings a rush of excitement. The people, the textbooks and backpacks, it all has this energy that I want to live inside forever. I find Blair on the first floor of the library in the campus tutor center.

"Hey!" She waves me over from her cubicle. A letterboard above her desk reads, *The future belongs to those who believe in the beauty of their dreams.*

"Look at you coming up with awesome, cheesy quotes." I sit down at the chair in front of her desk and pull the letterboard in front of me.

"Eleanor Roosevelt said that." She grabs her backpack and unzips the front pocket. "I have something for you."

"Oh yeah?"

She grins and pushes a piece of paper in front of me. An intricately folded paper star that's been colored yellow. "What is this?"

"It's your deflowering pin, of course."

I snort. "You're ridiculous."

"I was bored. It's been slow in here this week. No one cares about careers, they're just ready for summer break. So… tell me everything."

Blair hangs on every word. I give her the basic rundown of how my night went down. She'd helped with the candles and knew my intent, but she's smiling so big you'd think I won an Oscar instead of lost my virginity. The details, the things we said, the bond I'd felt, I leave all of that out. For one, I'm not ready to admit how Zeke makes me feel. And for two, it'll hurt a lot worse when he leaves if everyone is watching for me to break.

"So, where does that leave you two? Are you dating?"

"We're hanging out. Casual fun." I force an air of insignificance into my tone and avoid eye contact.

I can feel her intense stare and know she wants to say more, but I warn her off. "I don't want to make a big deal of it. We're just having fun until he leaves. I'll get to start my senior year with some experiences, just like I always wanted."

"Well, good. Actually, I'm glad to hear you say that. I don't want to see you get hurt."

"Exactly, me either." I sit straighter and force a big smile. "So, on to more important topics, I need your advice, not as my friend but as Valley's career resource expert."

"Shoot." She crosses her arms over her chest and sits back.

"I'm thinking about switching majors."

"To what?"

"I'm not sure."

"I don't understand." Her mouth pulls into a straight line, but her tone remains soft and understanding. "You're almost done with your business degree. You're not going to apply to the MBA program?"

"No, I'm not. Please don't be mad at me," I rush before I lose my nerve. "I didn't want to say anything until I was sure."

"I'm not mad. I'm sad we won't be taking the same classes, though. And who will I go into business with?"

"You don't need me or anyone else. You're going to rock a startup all on your own and I'll be there to cheer you on the whole way."

A real smile reaches her eyes. "What are you thinking of switching majors to?"

"Art, maybe, or marketing, I'm not sure. That's why I'm here, so you can help me figure it out."

Her eyes light up. "Ooooh, this could be fun."

Blair hooks me up with about a dozen different career placement tests and a stack of books on choosing a career.

"Want to come over tonight and drink wine while I uncover my perfect career?"

"I can't tonight. Tomorrow?"

"Sure, my future can wait until then." I stand. "Wanna grab lunch at University Hall?"

She looks around. "Why not. My shift goes for another ten minutes, but let's be honest, no one else is coming to see me today." Her phone pings. "It's Wes. I'm going to tell the guys to meet us there."

A little thrill at seeing Zeke shoots through me, which I ignore. "Cool."

We've just grabbed a table when they walk into University Hall. Wes slides in next to Blair and Zeke hovers at my side.

"Hey." I scoot over so he can take a seat.

It's awkward for all of two seconds until he places a large open palm on my leg and squeezes and drops his mouth to mine.

"Hey, beautiful," he murmurs as he pulls his lips away.

I'm certain I'm blushing, and I can feel Blair and Wes watching, but screw it. I wrap my arms around his neck, claiming him in front of whoever cares enough to see, and kiss him again. It's the last week of classes before finals, so our time hanging out like this on campus, or anywhere really, is closing in fast. I'm making the most of every opportunity.

"I can't stay," he says. "I promised Malone I'd meet him at the gym."

"Can I come watch you work out?"

"Sure. Prepare to be bored, though."

Bored watching him? Is he crazy? "I think I'll manage to stay entertained."

He grins, a boyish smile that may or may not make my stomach do a little flip. I'm pleading the fifth.

As we stand to leave, Blair calls after me. "Don't forget, Vanessa and I are moving our stuff in on Thursday morning."

"I won't forget. I may even carry a box or two."

She snorts. "I'm not holding my breath." Then she squeezes Wes' arm. "That's why I have a boyfriend. To lift heavy things and reach items on the top shelf."

At Ray Fieldhouse, I park myself on the sideline and pull out my economics textbook. I don't need to study for my online final exam, I know it backward and forwards, but if I just gawk at Zeke for the next couple hours, he might get creeped out. Still, it's hard to look away.

Malone uses some sort of pad like a shield and pushes against Zeke's back. Zeke has the ball and forces his way backward, shuffling his feet and spinning to try and get around Malone. Malone is fast and blocks Zeke at every turn. Power and determination etch Zeke's features. He's bigger than Malone and if they were under the basket could probably just shoot over his head, but Zeke never looks to take a shot, they just move up and down the court over and over until I'm tired just watching them work so hard.

The Tip-Off

I'm fending off a yawn when they call it. Zeke walks over to me, sweat dripping from him and a mischievous twinkle in his eye. He moves in to give me a sweaty bear hug. I shriek but don't really care. Actually, I think it's kinda hot.

"Did you just lick my chest?"

"Mayyybe."

"You never cease to amaze me."

"Is that a good thing?" I ask hopefully.

He grabs my bag from the floor and takes my hand. "Yeah, it's a good thing."

thirty-one

Zeke

We go to my place so I can get ready for my flight tomorrow. After a shower, I'm packing while Gabby sits on my bed with her laptop open in front of her. She's put on a pair of glasses that I've never seen her wear, but hello sexy librarian, and has a look of deep concentration.

"You studying?"

"Sort of," she responds without looking up.

I re-count the boxers and pairs of socks already in my bag and then toss in a hand full of workout gear. My suit is already in the garment bag hanging from the door so I don't forget it.

The combine lasts several days and selected players from all over the country will be there. Sara and I went back and forth about my going. It's an honor to be invited, only about sixty players total, but whereas it's an opportunity for some players to showcase their talents, it's also an opportunity for players to drop from a team's radar. It's almost all downside for me since I'm already getting the attention and consideration from teams, but I want to prove I'm worthy of the number one pick and I also want to show these teams that I've leaned out a bit. All those cardboard meals can't have been for naught.

"How flexible are you?"

"Decent." My mind goes to the flexibility and agility tests I'll be undergoing. I've practiced them over and over, I know I'm where I need to be, but until Sunday when I'm on a plane back to Valley, I'm not going to stop wondering if I've done enough and if it's a huge mistake to be going at all.

"Any preferences on standing versus sitting?"

I grab a pair of compression shorts and tights and add them to the bag. "Standing or sitting? What do you mean?"

I've got my back turned to her, setting my packed bag by the door when she answers. "For sex. I was thinking this looked fun, what do you think?"

I face her, processing the words as I do. Her blonde hair has fallen over one shoulder as she leans over the laptop that is now rotated so I can see the screen. She presses a button and suddenly my room is filled with cheesy porn music and some girl moaning like she's, well, a porn star. My gaze flies to the screen where a chick with giant boobs is being held against a wall by a creepy AF looking dude who pounds into her while simultaneously sucking a nipple.

When I can speak past my surprise, I ask, "What were the other options?" I'm hella curious what else she's been watching while I packed my bag completely oblivious.

Her eyes light up and she quickly navigates to another video. This one features the same chick. This time she's bouncing on a guy's lap. The dude, as creepy as the last one, is reclined back in a big La-Z-Boy chair and he's looking past her, presumably to a TV since instead of the porn music it's a football game announcer talking Green Bay stats.

"Or…" Again she takes control of the keyboard and switches to another video.

"Definitely no," I say and shake my head at the video of some sort of wheelbarrow sex. The chick looks miserable trying to hold up her own weight in a push-up position while the guy stands behind her, holding her thighs and driving into her. I'm all for mixing things up, but I don't want the girl I'm banging to be grimacing and counting the seconds until I come because there's no way she's getting off like that.

"Does that also mean no standing doggy style?"

She sounds so disappointed that I can't help but laugh. "You know what, we'll do whatever you want. We'll try them all if that's what you want."

"Really?"

"Yeah, it's gonna be a *real* burden, but I'll manage." I take the laptop, close it and set it on my desk. Then I join her on the bed and pull her onto my lap.

"Where should we start?" she asks as she wraps her arms around my neck.

"Could start with getting naked."

The Tip-Off

I left my shirt off after I showered so I'm most of the way there, but Gabby is wearing entirely too many clothes. I reach for the hem of her shirt and feel her stiffen. Shit, I completely forgot her hesitancy to take off her shirt. I've seen her scars, but I respect her desire to keep them covered during sex. As eager as she is to try it all, she's a constant contradiction of reckless and afraid. Eager and reserved.

So, I skip the shirt and draw her to me. I take her mouth and kiss her until she relaxes in my arms. Gabby kisses with her entire body. She presses into me and pulls me closer all while drinking me in with such desire it stirs a feeling inside of me that I've never felt. I like kissing her, bringing out the passion in her and giving it right back in turn.

When kissing isn't enough, I undo her shorts and she scoots off me so I can pull them down and then get rid of mine as well. I grab a condom from the nightstand and cover myself while she watches. When I'm done, she climbs back on me and lets out a little moan when my dick nudges at her pussy. She rises slightly and lines me up, sinking down before I'm sure she's ready.

"This angle is kind of intense. Go slow."

She nods once and rolls her bottom lip behind her teeth. Gradually she lowers herself onto me as I whisper encouragement and make sure she knows it's okay to give her body time to adjust. When she's taken me to the hilt, her body quivers.

"You're squeezing me like a vise. So damn tight," I mumble into the nape of her neck and kiss the sensitive spot just above her collarbone.

She lifts her hips slightly and then asks, "How am I

supposed to move like this?"

I move my hands to her hips and lift her inch by inch to the tip and then start to bring her down just as slowly. "You're not."

"Oooh," she says. "None of the work and all the enjoyment."

"That's right. Relax and let me make you feel good, sweetheart."

The position and the control I have over her body brings me close faster than I'd like. When I can't take it anymore, I lift her until my dick slips out and we both groan at the loss.

"Turn around," I instruct and then help her maneuver so she's facing away. "That's it. Now same thing, but this time move your feet up so they're underneath your knees and you can help set the tempo. If your legs get tired, then just lean back."

At first, we're out of sync, she's trying to go fast and I'm forcing her slow, but we're two ambitious people with a common goal and soon we're moving together, and I can feel her trembling around me and her breaths coming faster, moans are the soundtrack of the moment.

The position lacks the intimacy I dig with her, so I lift her shirt in the back to access some skin. I've just gotten it to the middle of her back when I see the scars from her side and realize they spread around on her back, too. I gently kiss her spine and increase the speed in which I lift and thrust into her.

I don't want it to be over. I want to be the guy who helps her discover every position, every sensation. "Ready to try standing?" I whisper in her ear.

She turns her head and looks at me, eyes wide. "Really?"

She scrambles off me and I stand and pull her from the bed. "How flexible are you?" I ask in a teasing voice, repeating the question she asked me earlier.

Instead of responding, she stands tall, sticks her butt as close to my crotch as she can and then bends over and grabs her ankles. Holy shit. My hands go to her ass and I squeeze. My dick twitches and begs for entry. I fist myself, position at her entrance and slide in, telling her how beautiful she is and how much I want her. Her responses come in the form of sighs and moans.

Her shirt gapes open in the front and I slide my hands underneath and cup her breasts over her bra. I'd give up a lot of things to feel her skin to skin right now.

As my thrusts grow harder, she has a hard time staying upright without toppling over so I quickly move us so she can lean onto the bed. Her face lays on the comforter, giving me a side view of every expression that crosses it. Pleasure. Excitement. Wonder. She's so fucking beautiful.

"I-I think I'm close," she rasps.

I increase the pace and sure enough, the walls of her pussy squeeze me and she calls out as the orgasm rips through her. My own release comes only seconds later, and I collapse onto the bed and pull her to me.

We lie like that until our breathing evens out.

"Thank God for porn," I mumble into the top of her head and breathe her in.

She snuggles closer and I feel her body shake with laughter. "I have so many ideas. You have no idea."

"I think I have a pretty good idea."

thirty-two

Gabby

Blair and Vanessa move their stuff from the sorority room they've shared for the past three years to our apartment. They don't have much in the way of living or kitchen stuff, so aside from their rooms finally being used, the only difference is the excitement it brings to the place. It's like the most epic slumber party ever that never has to end.

Wes and Mario have been here practically all day, something I realize quickly I'm going to have to get used to. I didn't just get two new roommates, I basically got four.

I try and picture what it'd be like if instead of being the fifth wheel, Zeke were here. The thought is pleasant until reality smacks me in the face. Regular classes are done, graduation is next weekend, and Zeke is leaving to go God knows where.

An incoming text pulls me from my thoughts and a spark of excitement jolts through me that Zeke has reached out. He left yesterday morning and aside from a text that he'd arrived, I haven't heard from him. Not that I expected to, it's just I miss him. God, I'm lame.

It's not Zeke, though, it's Nathan. We haven't hung out much since the lake and the funny memes he used to send almost daily have all but stopped. I've been giving him space in case that's what he needs, but I miss my friend.

Nathan: Party tonight at the rugby house. Come with? I miss my Gabs!

Me: Love to! Miss you too.

I excuse myself from the lovebirds and retreat to my bedroom. I have the mother of all headaches, probably from two nights with hardly any sleep. I pop a couple Motrin and head for the shower.

I take a little extra care with my hair, makeup, and wardrobe in hopes that'll put that extra bounce in my step tonight. I'm excited to hang with Nathan and desperately praying we can go back to being friends. I miss him, but with the pounding in my head not relenting, I'm starting to wish I could just stay in and take it easy tonight.

Nathan picks me up outside my apartment.

"Gabs!" he calls out of his open window. "Hop in."

Shaw leans forward from the passenger side and waves, a bottle of Seagram's 7 in the other hand.

"Hey, guys."

I get in the back and Shaw offers me the bottle which I wave off. "No thanks. I've got a killer headache."

Nathan drives us to a small house about a block away from the baseball house.

"Do all the jocks live around here?"

"The ones that don't live in the dorms," Shaw offers.

"I think I picked the wrong neighborhood to live in."

The music sounds twice as loud as usual and when Nathan offers me a cup, I shake my head. Shaw wanders off and I stick to Nathan's side. Nathan is well-known and well-liked, so we stop a lot to say hello to people. I'm even starting to recognize a few faces and be recognized, which is fun. I feel less like the awkward new girl.

"Wanna hit the dance floor?" Nathan asks and points to where people are dancing in the middle of the back yard.

"I don't think I'm up for it."

"I'm sorry. Anything I can do? Do you wanna go inside where it's quieter?"

His kindness makes me feel like a total buzzkill. "You know what, screw it." I grab his hand and pull him to the dance floor.

It's not my level best effort, but I find a rhythm that doesn't make the stabbing pain in the front of my head any worse.

"It's good to hang with you again," he says, leaning in so I can hear him over the music. "Sorry I screwed it up there for a while."

"You don't have anything to apologize for." I bite down on my lip and summon the courage to say the thing that's been on my mind since that night on the boat. "I'm sorry if I gave you the wrong idea. I love spending time with you, truly."

He stops my awkward ramblings. "You didn't. I just got caught up in all the coupling up going on at The White House. First Wes, then Joel. Everyone is settling down."

"*You* want a girlfriend?"

He blushes, grabs my hand, and spins me around to the beat of the song. "Is that so surprising?"

"Actually, yes. You spend every night partying and drinking, which is totally fine, but it doesn't exactly scream 'I'm ready to settle down.'"

His jaw flexes and he nods. Before I can comment further on his love life, he turns the tables on me. "What about you and Zeke? I swear I never thought I'd see the day that guy cared about anything but ball."

"It's casual," I insist and turn to the side so he can't see the blush on my face.

"Maybe, but it's been a trip to see Zeke get knocked on his ass."

"Have you heard from him since he left?"

"No. I doubt he's had time to even look at his phone. The combine is intense. The guys get measured, weighed, they run drills, scrimmage. All in front of coaches and scouts from every NBA team in the league. It's gotta be extra intense for Zeke coming in as the expected number one pick. Everyone is gunning for him. It's lonely at the top – or so I hear."

I realize I haven't bothered to ask Zeke a lot of questions about everything happening with him. Our interactions have been all about me and things I want to do. He said that just because what we're doing is casual that it was still special and he was right, but I've done a shitty job of showing it.

Simone dances up beside us and Nathan and I pull back so we can say hello. She wraps her arms around his neck, and they hug. The moment to myself allows my headache to remind me it's still very much there. Also, I really want to go call Zeke. Even if I have to leave a message, I want to tell him I'm proud of him and excited for his future. He deserves to hear that.

"Hey, Nathan." I tug on his arm and flash Simone a smile. "I'm gonna take off. This headache won't give up."

"Do you want me to come with?"

"No, of course not. Stay and enjoy the party. I'm just gonna go home and go to bed. I'll call you tomorrow."

I get two steps away when I pull out my phone and realize the battery is dead. Nathan and Simone are still in the same spot, so I interrupt them again. "Sorry, my phone is dead. Can I use yours to call a ride?"

Nathan pulls his keys from his front jeans pocket. "Take my car."

I hesitate and he presses them into my hand. I mumble my thanks and he turns back to Simone completely oblivious to the war in my head. Blair and Z are the only ones that know I don't drive. Honestly, it's not a hard thing to avoid when everyone is always piling in together or taking an Uber.

As I walk out of the party and toward Nathan's car, the keys feel heavy in my hand. I weigh my options. I could run back inside, borrow a phone and call a cab, or hell, I could call Blair, she'd come, I know she would, but it's starting to feel a little pathetic having her chauffeur me around.

Inhaling and letting out a deep breath, I unlock the car and get in. I make all the necessary adjustments to the seat and the mirrors and then start the engine. The music is blasting from our drive over and I turn it off so I can focus. No distractions.

"You can do this. It's like riding a bike," I talk to myself out loud in the empty car.

Before I can psych myself out, I put it in drive and pull away from the curb. My heart races and I focus on breathing. I don't even look at the speedometer to know I'm going well below the twenty-five mile per hour limit.

There aren't a lot of cars out so the closer I get to my place, the more I relax. I start to smile when I'm in the final mile. Only one stoplight is between me and my final destination and it's green. Feels like a literal sign that I should be going for it more.

I can't wait to get home and call Zeke. I want to ask him all about his day and tell him I drove. I can almost hear his voice congratulating me. I don't know why making Zeke proud fills me with such happiness, but I'm not about to dissect it now. Ten and two, Gabby.

The light turns yellow right before I get to the intersection and I hesitate, panic taking over as I try and decide between slamming on the brakes and increasing my speed. At the last second, I decide on the first. The car skids to a stop as the light turns red and I let out a shaky breath of relief. But only for a second do I breathe easy. Squealing tires has my body going rigid and I brace for the impact my brain hasn't even acknowledged. And then everything moves forward.

thirty-three

Zeke

"If the number of times I was told how good you looked is any indication, I think it's going well."

Sara is excited, which tells me I've done my job. She talks animatedly with her hands, her third cup of coffee sitting on the table between us. My days since arriving in Chicago for the combine have been long and grueling, but Sara's been there every step and staying up even later to make sure I get face time with teams.

"New York has the first pick, Denver the second. You have a meeting with both of them tomorrow morning and with the Suns in the afternoon. I've also set up meetings with other teams, but I think it's unlikely you'll go any later than top three. New York and Denver both could use someone with your size, plus the hype around getting the all-around top pick gives their teams a boost. Any questions?"

I shake my head. Even that feels like it takes too much energy. I'm bone-tired and already looking forward to falling into bed and sleeping for a hundred years. Or five hours since that's all I'm going to get.

"Really good work today, Zeke."

I don't remember the walk or the ride up the elevator, but when my head hits the pillow, I groan in satisfaction. I kick off my shoes and don't even bother changing out of my sweaty workout clothes. Sleep is more important than a shower right now.

My cell buzzes but I don't move. I know the guys are probably curious how today went, but I'll text Wes in the morning. The second time it buzzes, I curse my nosey roommates but reach out for it without opening my eyes and fumble around until my fingers wrap around the device. I bring it to my face before I force my lids open just a crack. Hell, I've got twenty-two texts and ten missed calls. I'm reading the first text from Wes that says to call him when my phone rings. The fact that it's Nathan is enough to rouse my sleep fogged brain. Alarm bells are going off and I sit up and answer the phone.

"Nate? What's going on, man?"

thirty-four

Gabby

I don't like hospitals. Not that anyone really does, but my fear is rooted from waking up four years ago not remembering my friends or family and staring back at a face that I didn't recognize. The memory loss was temporary, but the scary reality of how close I came to dying is a constant presence. It impacts everything I do without me even consciously aware that I'm doing it. Although, right now, I'm fully aware that I never want to get behind the wheel of a car again.

Blair comes around the corner of the curtain pulled in front of the bed I'm sitting on inside the emergency room with wide eyes. "Thank God."

She squeezes me hard and I wince. "Easy there."

"Sorry." She pulls back and eyes my bandaged wrist. "Wes and Nathan are in the waiting room and your mom wants you to call her as soon as we get home."

"You called my mom?!" I hop off the table and groan. "On a scale from one to ten, how nuts did she sound?"

"Eleven."

"If she shows up at our apartment, I'm going to kill you."

I use Blair's phone to call my mom on the ride home. I close my eyes and listen to her sob. I promise to call if I need anything, to take it easy, and to be careful. The last one is a signature promise that she demands every time we talk. In return, she promises not to come, and I relax a bit as we hang up the phone.

"Okay, tiny step up here," Blair's voice is bordering condescending as she helps me into our apartment. Behind her, Nathan has a hand at my back like I might topple over at any moment. Oh, and don't worry, Wes is in front guiding me like I've gone blind instead of broken my wrist.

"You guys are being ridiculous, I'm fine." I move my hands up above my head and shake my body as if to prove my point, but a stab of pain causes me to wince and I give in and let Blair drag me to the couch.

"Try and keep it elevated as much as possible. It'll help with the swelling," Wes says, offering me a sympathetic smile.

"I've got this, really. This is nothing compared to…" My words trail off and the memory of what rough shape I was in after the last accident causes me to hold my tongue.

"Do you need anything before bed? I could help you get changed or do you want me to sleep with you?"

I have to laugh at her stubborn but loyal will. "I'm okay, Blair. Honest. I'm gonna hang out here for a few minutes and then go to bed."

She doesn't move for a moment, just stares at me gauging my ability to manage on my own. She steps to me quickly and wraps me in a tight hug. "I'm sorry I'm being a mother hen, but I was so scared. I love you, Gabs."

"Me too," I whisper, emotions clogging my throat. I refuse to cry. I am not opening those floodgates and taking a ride on the pity express.

When she finally releases me and heads to her room, Nathan takes a seat next to me. He was quiet the whole way back from the hospital. Guilt practically seeps from him like the alcohol I can smell. I rest my head on his shoulder. "Sorry about your car."

"Stop apologizing. It was a piece of shit anyway. I should have been with you. I never would have let you drive home by yourself if I'd known." His mouth pulls into a tight line. "If I'd known you hadn't driven since the accident."

"I was trying to prove that I'm a big girl who can take care of myself. Fitting, right?"

He wraps his arms around me and squeezes lightly. I pull away and yawn. "I should get some sleep. Vanessa is at Mario's if you want to take her bed."

"Nah, I'm good on the couch." As if to prove it, he lies down and cocks his arm behind his head.

After I grab him a blanket and pillow, I shut myself in my room and awkwardly attempt to lift my dress over my head. "Curse you Spandex."

I'm breathing heavy by the time I get one arm

through the dress, so I say screw it to changing for bed and climb under the covers with my dress up around my chest. Despite how tired I am, sleep doesn't come easily. The only plus side, the throbbing of my wrist has made the headache pale in comparison.

Every time I close my eyes, I hear the squealing of tires and the crunch of the back of Nathan's car when I was rear-ended. My heart races and I push the tears back. I will not go there. It took me so long to move on last time and I don't want to spend another four years recovering from this one. It was an accident. Accidents happen. I'm okay. I'm okay.

I'm okay.

Zeke

The front door is unlocked, so I slip inside Gabby's apartment and spot Nathan sleeping on the couch. I move as quietly as possible to her room. For the first time since I got the call from Nathan that she'd been in a car accident, my lungs fill with air.

I slip off my shoes and climb in behind her and pull her into my arms. She turns to me and slowly opens her eyes. She smiles, closes her eyes, and then as if just realizing I'm here, they fly back open. She throws an arm around me, hitting me in the head with the cast in the process. We both wince, but I hug her tightly.

"What are you doing here?"

"I came as soon as I heard. Are you okay?"

She nods, but soon I can feel her shoulders shake and when I pull back and tilt her head up to see her face, tears run down her cheeks.

"Hey, hey, shhh." I wipe her tears and then bring her head back to my chest. I rub her back and shoulders until my hands snag on the material caught around her neck. "Whatcha got going on here?"

"I-I c-couldn't get my dress off." She cries harder.

I bite back a laugh as I help her out of the dress and toss it on the floor. "Do you want me to grab a shirt for you?"

She shakes her head and then pulls at mine.

The laugh escapes this time, but I yank my shirt off and gingerly pull it over her head and get her arms through. "That shirt probably smells as bad as I do. I haven't showered in almost twenty-four hours and there was a lot of sweating between then and now."

"I like your sweaty smell." She sniffles, the tears coming slower now. "How was the combine? Is it over already? I thought you were staying 'til Sunday."

"It was great." My chest squeezes. I don't know what the repercussions are going to be for walking out like I did, but I can't think about that now. "I left a little early so I could check on you. It's all good." *I hope.*

She yawns. "I wanna hear all about it." Her eyelids flutter closed, and she nuzzles into my chest.

"I'll tell you all about it tomorrow," I whisper. "Get some sleep, Gabby. I'm here."

thirty-five

Zeke

"I'm sorry, did you just say you left *before* your interviews with the teams? That sounds bad. Like you flaked on a job interview. What did Sara say?" Gabby pauses the movie and turns to face me.

After getting in early this morning, we slept late, and I haven't been able to pry myself out the door yet. I did manage to shower, though, and Wes brought me over some clean clothes, so I have absolutely no reason to leave. I haven't taken a day off working out in years. I'm cashing in on all those bonus workouts I did, and I can't imagine a better way to spend it than with Gabby.

"She's…" I move my head from side to side to come up with a better word than pissed. My phone has been buzzing pretty much nonstop with text updates to the mess I made. "Dealing with it. She told the teams I had a family emergency and she's trying to set up times with teams individually."

"Zeke, oh my God. Why did you do that? After everything you've worked for." Her eyes search mine for an explanation.

There's only about a foot of space between us on the couch, but I close the distance and take her good hand in mine. "I didn't think. Just grabbed my bag and headed to the airport and got on the first plane out. I wanted to be here for you, knew it had to be hard, and if I'm honest, I guess I felt a little responsible after pushing you to drive again."

"Are you kidding me? Do you know how huge it is that I finally drove? Years of therapy didn't do half as much for me as you have."

"Does that mean you're going to try again?"

"Absolutely not. Nope. Never." She chuckles. "I'm strictly a passenger from now on. In fact, I may just start biking everywhere. I'll get one of those cute ones with the basket in front."

"I bet you'd look pretty hot riding a bike around town."

"Yeah?" She climbs into my lap.

"Mhmm. Tan legs, blonde hair blowing in the wind, and don't forget about the adorable pink helmet to protect that pretty head of yours." I cup her face and then kiss the top of her head.

She leans into me so we're chest to chest. "Tell me more about the combine."

We sit like that. I play with her hair and answer questions as she fires them off. I tell her everything, about the skills testing, the scrimmages. She asks about some of the other prospects that were there, and I'm surprised when she's even done her homework to know which teams get the top picks this year. I leave out the worry that my leaving like I did cost me a shot at my dream, but what I told her was true. I didn't think – just knew I had to get to her.

Sara calls a little later and Gabby goes to lie down while I take the call in the living room.

"Well, I got your interviews rescheduled with Denver and the Suns. New York hasn't gotten back to me yet." I can hear her exasperation. She's been working her ass off for me, and I just made her job twice as hard. "I'm sending all the information to your email."

"Thank you. I really appreciate it. I'm sorry."

"For blowing off the men and women who control your future or for giving me an ulcer?" Her laugh is small, but it makes me feel a tiny bit better.

"The second one."

"Just, promise me you're going to be on that flight to Denver on Monday."

"I promise."

I open my email and look at the meetings Sara was able to reschedule. Between those and my trip home to see my mom, the next month is going to be chaotic. I tuck my phone into my pocket and go to find Gabby. She's lying in bed, but instead of sleeping, she's got her phone in front of her face. When she sees me, she sets it down and sits up, leaning on one elbow. "Everything okay?"

"Yeah, Sara got the meetings rescheduled."

"Good." She visibly relaxes.

I slide into bed beside her and pull her carefully on

top of me. "How's your wrist?"

"It's fine."

"Good because I leave Monday morning and I want to spend every second I have left in Valley kissing you."

"What does that have to do with my wrist?"

I grab her good arm and pin it above her head. "It's never just kissing with you."

She brings her lips to mine, proving my point by grinding against me with her lower half in the process. Kissing turns to groping over clothes, but neither of us pushes for more right away. We're savoring every minute. I'm memorizing her face and the sounds she makes when she's happy, a little contented sigh, and the feelings that doing this brings out in me. I never want to forget any of it.

I've finally got my hand up her shirt when Vanessa gets home and calls out to see if anyone else is here.

"Shit, I forgot to close the door," I say, pulling back and eyeing the open bedroom door.

"I got it," she says. She walks to the door, says hello to Vanessa and then adds, "We're about to have sex, so I'm gonna shut this, okay?"

A laugh rumbles in my chest and Gabby shuts the door and then presses her back against it eyeing me with a look of pure want and desire. I'm on my feet. I can't wait one more second for her to be in my arms again.

I fist her shirt and use it to pull her to me. I lean in to kiss her, but she pulls away. "Wait." She takes a deep breath and lets it out slowly. "I know you've seen the scars on my stomach, but…" Her chest heaves with breaths coming fast and ragged. "They're all over my body." She waves a hand down her left side. "If this is our last weekend together, I want to be with you. Really be with you, with nothing between us, but I don't want you to be surprised by just how extensive the scarring is, and if it's too much for you to deal with, I'll understand."

A vise squeezes my heart. "I don't care about the scars."

"You're a good guy, Zeke, and I know you'd never cut and run or leave me hanging, but I don't want this to turn into a pity fuck."

"Are you serious right now?" My voice comes out louder than I'd intended. Hot rage bubbles inside me that she could believe I'm capable of doing such a thing. Can she not see how crazy I am about her?

I lower my voice. "Listen to me, you are not a pity fuck. Not to me and not for any other guy out there. You are beautiful inside and out. Those aren't just words, they're facts."

"You're just saying that because you're about to get laid." She laughs, a hollow, brittle sound.

"No, I'm really not." I run the pad of my thumb delicately across the scars on her face. "You are beautiful. Not in spite of the scars, but because of them."

She rolls her eyes. "If you tell me they make me unique and special, I swear to you I will throw myself out the window."

"You live on the ground level."

Her brow arches and I chuckle as I search for words to make her believe that when I look at her, I don't try and see past the scars, I don't even avoid looking at them. They're part of her. Maybe not a part she likes, but they make up the person I know as Gabby and I don't secretly wish she were any different than she is.

"You know what I love most about them?" I bring both hands to her waist and lift the shirt over her head. Next, I unclasp her bra and slide the straps down her arms.

"What?" The whisper of the question comes as the lacy black material hits the floor.

Her nipples are a soft pink that tighten into buds when I follow the path of the scars on her stomach up to where one particularly large one ends on the side of her left breast.

"They mean that you lived. You're here with me right now. If you think that your scars make me want you any less, you're wrong. I want you because of them. I want you because you're here and you've made me feel more alive in the past month than I have my entire life. You lived and you brought me to life."

I try and make her feel and believe with my touch. Soft caresses of her skin. Light kisses trailing over her collarbone and down. I undo the button of her shorts with trembling hands. There's only this small piece of denim material keeping me from seeing all of her. She takes the initiative and pushes them down. I'm a goner, unable to look anywhere but at her and I'm definitely not subtle about my appreciation.

I take a step back and just keep right on staring at her, wondering how I got so lucky and imagining all the ways I want to show and prove to her that I'm not lying when I say I think she's beautiful. No, not just beautiful. The most beautiful thing I've ever seen.

In basketball, we refer to this moment as the triple

threat. It's when a player first gets possession of the ball and can pass, shoot, or dribble. The full range of offensive options are at his disposal. For five seconds, he can question which move to make, but after that, after he makes a move, the options dwindle. Do nothing and he turns the ball over to the other team. Five perfect seconds under pressure to make a decision that can make or break an offense.

This moment feels just like that and I consider my options carefully.

One Mississippi.

Two Mississippi.

Three Mississippi.

Four Mississippi.

thirty-six

Gabby

My chest heaves and I suck in a breath while Zeke stares at me. Before the accident, I derived my self-worth, at least in part, from being a beautiful and outgoing girl. Since then, I've battled the things people say against the reality of how I feel. People tell me beauty is skin deep. They're wrong. The longing I feel to be seen as beautiful is rooted deep in my soul.

Right now, I believe I am.

"Lie on the bed." His voice is deep and thick with emotion.

He pulls the shirt over his head and pushes his shorts and boxers to the floor. When he stands tall, nearly seven feet of muscled perfection, I'm drawn to him in a way that has nothing to do with the way he looks, and I wonder if it's the same for him.

I hope so... and also not. I want him to want me because he thinks I'm beautiful, but I don't want him to ignore the ugly either. I want someone to love me for the ugly and the beautiful, and every shade in between. True vulnerability is being seen for everything you are, the good and the bad, and Zeke is the first person I've let see every part of me. The fact that he seems to like me, just the way I am, is breathtaking and terrifying all at once.

He starts at my feet, dropping kisses to my ankle and moving up slowly, not skipping an inch of skin. He does the same to the other leg before he climbs on top of me and takes my mouth in the softest and sweetest caress, tracing my lips with his fingers and then his tongue.

Threading his hands through my hair at the nape of my neck, he pulls my hair away from my face and gazes into my eyes.

"Are we gonna have sex now, big guy, or what?" My voice comes out sounding small, the humor I'd meant to inflict not quite hitting the mark.

"Don't rush me, beautiful girl." He smirks and grinds his erection against my hip. He brushes a quick kiss on my lips and then pushes himself up so he's hovering over me. "I gotta get a condom."

"Wait." I wrap my arms around him to keep him from leaving. "I'm on birth control."

"Good." Is his only response before dropping his mouth to take my left nipple into his mouth.

I squeeze my eyes closed so I don't have to see his perfect mouth against the scars that wrap around the sensitive mound.

"Hey," he whispers. "Open your eyes." He takes my

nipple again, sucks and then lets it free with a pop. "Just watch me."

By the time Zeke finishes kissing literally every inch of my body, I'm practically feverish with my need to come. With his eyes locked on mine, he pushes inside of me, and I watch as his face contorts with the same mixture of contentment and a desire for more. So much more.

I'm spinning so fast. Pleasure mixed with emotion makes my orgasm rise to the surface so quickly we're just getting started and I'm already so close.

"You're so fucking beautiful, Gabby." The words come whispered into my ear and I believe him. That belief takes me over the edge, and I respond by screaming his name over and over like a prayer.

thirty-seven

Gabby

"Movie room in five." Joel peeks his head into Zeke's room and then dashes away.

"Your room looks so sad." Everything Zeke owns, save a change of clothes for tomorrow, is packed in boxes. He's not officially moving his things out until he knows where he's going and gets a place, but the room is as good as empty and tomorrow he'll be gone. "Now that you and Wes are moving out, who'll move in?"

"I'm not sure. It's weird to think about a new group of guys moving in." He zips up the last bag and tosses it on the floor. "I guess that's it." He takes a long look around the room and then extends a hand. "Ready for movie night?"

Everyone else is already there when we walk into the movie room. Nathan, Wes, Blair, Katrina, and Joel are all crowded inside. Joel has a bottle of champagne in hand and pops the cork, claiming it's cause for a classy celebration. When he drinks directly from the bottle, I have to laugh. Classy celebration isn't really their style anyway.

Joel wipes his mouth with the back of his hand and passes the bottle to Zeke. "For our last movie night—"

Zeke groans. "For the *last* time, I'm not dying." But he's smiling as he takes a long drink and then hands the champagne to me. Before I can bring it to my lips, he leans in and kisses me, giving me a hint of the sweet liquid he's drunk.

When we've all had our celebratory drink directly from the bottle, Joel holds the bottle up and everyone goes quiet.

"It's been a wild three years, two together in this house. You guys are more than roommates, more than teammates, more than friends." He pauses and looks like he's fighting back real emotion. "We're brothers and I'm going to miss the hell out of you two." Clearing his throat, he turns to the TV. "In honor of our la— our final movie night as roommates, I thought we should take it back old school. *Top Gun.*"

There are exactly enough chairs for all of us, but Zeke pulls me onto his lap, and I curl up so every inch of my body is touching him, soaking up every bit of him I can. I'd been told that movie night was sacred and that talking was strictly prohibited, but there's no stopping the laughing and quoting the movie at nearly every scene.

I've seen the movie before so I spend it watching Zeke's reaction to the film.

"This one is your favorite?"

He nods proudly.

"Why do you like Tom Cruise so much anyway?"

"My dad liked Tom Cruise. He'd always say, 'When I'm directing Tom, then I'll know I've made it.' Tom became an ideal in my mind. Even after my dad left, maybe more so, Tom represented something – achieving my goals, I guess. Plus, he's awesome."

"Did he ever get to direct Tom?"

Zeke shakes his head. "No."

"Do you talk to your dad often?"

"Not since he left. He tried a couple times – once recently after we won the tournament, but I never call him back. He made his choice to have a career instead of a family. There's no going back from that. He was right, you can't have both." He shrugs off the importance of that statement and my stomach knots.

But when Zeke leans in so his lips hover near my ear and sings along softly as Maverick serenades Charlie, I push thoughts of anything but the present and enjoying this night far away.

After the movie, he says his goodbyes to the guys, and we head upstairs. I've never given much thought to the difference between having sex versus making love, but I think it's the latter we're doing as Zeke undresses me, kissing me so sweetly, and taking his time bringing us both to orgasm.

"I'm going to miss you," he says when we're lying together afterward. His flight is early in the morning, so there will be no time then to say our goodbyes.

"Me too." I turn so we're spooning and wrap his arm tightly around my waist. "Thank you for... well just thank you. These past few weeks have meant so much to me. I'll never forget them, or you."

He squeezes me playfully. "You sound like Joel. I'm not dying. I'll see you when I come back to get my stuff. Plus, there's always phone sex."

I laugh, but purely for his benefit. I don't feel anything but sad that he's leaving, and I can't tell him that or it sounds like I'm not excited for his future.

"Before I forget, I got you something. It's waiting at your apartment for you." He yawns and a not a minute later his breathing evens out.

I don't know how long it takes me to fall asleep. I lie as still as I can so I don't wake him and cry silent tears.

The next morning we're both bleary-eyed as he drops me at my apartment before his flight. He jogs around to the passenger side door and opens it for me. I wrap my arms around him tightly and lean up on my tiptoes until he gets the hint and picks me up so I can wrap my arms around his neck and kiss him like it's the last time. I hope it's not.

"Stay out of trouble without me," he calls as he gets back in his car. I watch him drive away and then walk into my apartment finally letting the loud sobs wrack my body. It's so stupid. I don't even know why I'm sad. Casual fun isn't supposed to end in heartbreak.

Inside my room, I stop short at the pink bike with a big red bow stuck to the basket, just like I said I wanted.

The Tip-Off

A card pokes out of the basket and I grab it and sit on the bed, reading through the sobs: *Someday I'm going to buy you a cherry red convertible. Until then… Zeke*

thirty-eight

Gabby
Three Weeks Later

I stop in the middle of campus and sit on the ledge of the fountain that is at the heart of the quad. The hot concrete scalds my legs, but it can't dim my excitement for this day. Not the one hundred and five temp that makes breathing difficult or the tiny bit of loneliness I'm not admitting to since Zeke left.

My summer classes started today and being at Valley U as a real student is everything I'd ever dreamed of. No, it's more. I'm taking an art class and a marketing class, trying to broaden my horizons with some classes in subjects I've always enjoyed but not considered as a career.

I'm going to finish up my business degree since I'm so close, but I'm leaning toward switching to art as my major. Or marketing. Clearly, I'm still undecided.

Blair sent a text that she and Vanessa are at The White House swimming, so instead of going home to get ready for work, I ride my bike there.

"I thought you didn't live here anymore," I tease Wes as I walk out to the pool.

"I've got a standing invitation as long as I bring booze or girls when I come." He lifts the beer in his hand and points to Blair. "I brought both."

Joel agrees with him, which earns an eye roll from Katrina. He's all talk, though, the way he looks at her and her son, it's clear they are it for him.

I slip off my shoes and sit by the pool, dipping my feet into the cool water. "Oh man, that feels great. It's so freaking hot today."

Wes takes a seat next to me and offers me a beer. "Thanks."

The cold liquid helps to bring my body temp back down. I have to be at work in an hour, so I sip slowly knowing it'll be my only one.

"Talked to Zeke?"

Heat that is not entirely the sun's fault blooms in my cheeks. "Yeah. He's in Illinois visiting his mom and extended family and tomorrow he flies to LA."

In truth, we've talked every day either by text or an actual phone conversation, and one video call from his hotel room in Denver that involved lotion as lube and a memory that is forever burned into my brain. Watching a guy get himself off is seriously hot.

"Joel's family is hosting the draft party next week. It'll be good to see him."

"They are?" I'm a little hurt that in all our

conversations, he didn't think to tell me.

"Oh shit. I'm not sure I was supposed to tell you that." He rubs a hand over his jaw. "Too late now, I guess. Act surprised when he tells you."

"I thought the draft was in New York?"

"It is, but you know Zeke isn't much for the spotlight unless he's on the court, so he wanted something a little more low key. I have a feeling if Joel's family hadn't offered, he would have watched the draft from his phone while practicing somewhere."

I have so many questions I want to ask, but Blair swims up to the side and the conversation turns to their nightly plans.

"I should go," I tell them. "I need to change before work. Is it cool if I use Zeke's old room?" I motion behind me.

With their approval, I set off toward Zeke's room. The door is closed and when I open it and step inside, his scent wraps around me. I sit on his unmade bed, the bare mattress a reminder that he's really gone and lie back and fish my phone out of my pocket.

Me: I'm in your room. It still smells like you.

Zeke: Good. Stay right where you are. I'll be there next week.

Me: So I've heard. When do you get in?

Zeke: Wednesday night. Be there at say, eight o'clock?

Me: With bells on.

Zeke: Better be the only thing you have on.

Zeke

"Who are you texting and is that a smile on your face?" My mom places the casserole dish in the middle of our kitchen table at precisely six o'clock. It's been the same way my entire life. Always exactly at six.

"Just a friend from Valley."

"You didn't tell me you were dating anyone." She takes a seat across from me with two plates and pushes one in front of me.

I spoon two large servings of her chicken surprise casserole onto my plate, thankful I don't have to count calories anymore and pick up my fork before I answer her. "It's not really like that."

"Don't tell me you're stringing some girl around with that whole friends with benefits crap."

"Mooom."

"I'm serious. I raised you better than that."

"It's just complicated. She's still at Valley and I don't know where I'm going to end up yet."

"So you and Gabby aren't going to try long-distance?"

I choke around the mouthful of chicken and it's the longest thirty seconds ever as I chug water and compose myself, my mother looking on with a smug smile. "How do you know about Gabby?"

"Instagram, of course."

"*You're* on Instagram?"

She rolls her eyes. "You say that like I'm a hundred years old. She seems sweet. How did you meet her?"

"She's Wes' girl's best friend."

"Ah, how is Wes? I always liked him."

Thankful for the topic change, I smile. "He's good. He's going to be coaching at Valley next year and he seems excited about that."

We eat in silence for several minutes before I drop my fork to my plate and prepare to ask my mother the question that's been plaguing me for weeks. "Do you think Dad had it right that you can't have a family and a successful career?"

"Whatever made you think he believed that?"

"I heard him. The day he left, you two were arguing and he said he needed to move closer to where the jobs were and that if he wanted to make it big, he couldn't be worrying about getting home to have dinner with us at six every night." I remember every detail of that night. The blue polo shirt he wore, the goatee he was sporting, and the devastated look on my mother's face.

"I didn't know you heard that. I'm sorry that you did. I can't imagine what you must have thought all these years."

"Well, he wasn't wrong. He *did* become successful and if I've learned anything the past few years, it's that it takes a lot of hours and sacrifices to have that kind of success. I know you managed it both, but you turned down better jobs so you could be here for me at night, drive me back and forth to practices and games."

"And I'd do it again in a heartbeat."

"So, you either sacrifice career or family?"

"It's not a sacrifice, honey, it's prioritizing what's important to you."

I mull that over wondering if it's that simple. Did my dad just not give a shit? Was it so easy to put career first because he didn't love me like my mom does?

"Do you think Dad would have been as successful if he'd stayed here with us and we'd been a real family?"

"I don't know. It would have been harder, probably, but I don't think your dad believed that it was a choice between career and family any more than I do."

"Why do you say that?"

She sighs and a flash of sadness crosses her face. This trip down memory lane is hard for her, and I regret putting her through it again, but I have to know if I've had it all wrong.

"I quit blaming myself." I swallow, throat thick with emotion, and meet her eyes. "Or you for him leaving a long time ago, so whatever you have to say doesn't matter. I just need to know."

Reaching across the table, she grabs my hand and squeezes. "Because he never once asked me to come with him."

"Would you have?"

"I can't say for sure, but when he started looking for jobs, it was all about him and what he wanted and needed. It was never a discussion of finding a new school for you or a job for me, it was all about him and what he needed to do. You deserved a father that showed you how to have both because I believe it is possible, don't you? Look where you are, about to be drafted to the NBA and you've got family."

"I know. I'm sorry I've been bad about calling and coming to see you since I went to college. I'll try and do a better job once I get settled."

"Good, I won't have to get my updates from social media, but I was talking about your teammates. They've always been like a family to you."

"Yeah, I guess so."

"I love you. I'd do anything for you, but I don't look back on my life and think of it as a sacrifice. A job is just a job. The people in your life are what makes it worth living. So, tell me about the rest of the guys. How's Nathan doing?"

I fill my mom in on all the rest of my roommates as we eat and then clean up the kitchen. It's late by the time I lie down on my childhood bed surrounded by trophies and ribbons from every sporting event I ever participated in, posters of Magic Johnson and Kobe Bryant, and newspaper clippings with my name splashed across the headline. After I went to college, my mom made a point to keep it exactly like it was. Even after the first year when I only came home once, she insisted it didn't matter how often I used it, just that it was here when I did.

I used to think when I made it to the NBA, I'd surprise her with a brand-new fancy-ass house or car, but I think she might kick my ass if I do that. Instead, I think I'll just add a big chunk of change to her bank account. I'm finally going to be able to repay her for not

The Tip-Off

being as selfish as my father and for just… everything.

thirty-nine

Zeke

Playing basketball was never about fame or money, or anything really except for the feeling like it was where I belonged. I've played in hundreds of basketball games, but it never gets old. The adrenaline, the grueling mental and physical stress, the wins and even the losses — I've loved every second of all of it.

Today is the NBA draft and I've imagined this day, every day, for the past four years. Maybe longer.

"The cameras won't go live until they announce your name. I think you'll go number two or three. New York hasn't given me a great feeling since the combine."

Burned that bridge. I wish I could say it hadn't been worth it, but that'd just be a straight-up lie.

I catch sight of Gabby across the room talking to Blair. She looks even more nervous than I feel. She catches my eye and lifts her champagne to me with a smile.

"Excuse me. I'll be right back."

Sara's staring at her phone, so she just nods as I step away. "Draft starts in five minutes."

"Hey, can I steal her?" I ask Blair and reach for Gabby.

In answer to my question, Blair reaches up and places a kiss on my cheek and walks away.

"Fancy event you got here." Gabby hoists the flute up again.

"Joel can't keep anything simple."

"Are you nervous?"

"A little."

Gabby places her hand in mine and tips her head to the left. "Have you talked to Nathan?"

I glance in that direction to see Nathan holding up a wall with a bottle of water in his hands. "Nah, not in a few weeks. Is he okay? I don't think I've ever seen him so subdued at a party."

"Bros before hos. I can't tell you or I'd be violating friendship code."

I lift a brow. "Did you just call me a ho?"

"Okay, I'm telling you this only because he never will, but if he asks it wasn't me that told you."

I nod in agreement.

"He's sad you're leaving. I don't know what all went down between you two, but I think he needs to know you aren't going to run off and forget about him."

I'm skeptical that's it, but I don't contradict her. "Alright. I'll talk to him."

She looks at me with a blank expression like she's

calling my bluff.

"Alright, alright. I'll talk to him right now."

She kisses my cheek. "You're a good guy, Zeke."

I watch her walk off before I amble toward him. "What's happening, man?"

"Hey!" He straightens and plasters a smile on his face. "Congratulations. The big day is finally here."

"Yeah, finally. What's new with you?" I'm cursing Gabby as we both stand here awkward as hell making small talk.

Nathan narrows his gaze and tilts his head up at me. "Why are you being weird?" I look to Gabby and he follows my gaze. "She put you up to this?"

"She might have mentioned you seemed a little off."

He shakes his head. "I'm fine. Gabby is making something out of nothing. You don't have to feel obligated to check in on me just because Gabby is worried."

"I don't feel obligated at all."

"I'm good. Really."

"Alright. I'll take your word for it." I look to Gabby. "How's she been? Wild and crazy as ever?"

"Gabby?" Nathan shakes his head. "Nah, not really. She's taking some classes on campus and working a lot. I think wild Gabby left when you did."

The thought that she's not still crossing items off her list makes me sad, though I can't say I'm not glad she's keeping out of trouble when I'm not there to look out for her.

Sara calls my name from across the room and motions me toward her.

"Looks like it's time for your big moment."

"Guess so." I take a step and then pause. "Come with me. My mom isn't here and Gabby refuses to be on camera, it'd be nice to have someone sitting next to me when they call my name."

"Seriously? Won't Sara and the camera guy be annoyed to have some nobody in the shot with you?"

"Not a nobody." I put my arm around his shoulder and squeeze. "My former teammate and friend."

If you'd asked me a year ago what the first thing I'd do after being selected third in the NBA Draft I would have said, *first off why wasn't I the first or second pick and secondly, what time does practice start?* But when the commissioner calls my name, the room erupts in cheers and I can't move.

The guy holding the camera steps closer, Nathan bumps my shoulder and screams, "Hell yeah!" and Sara tosses a Suns hat on my head and thrusts a jersey in my direction. I don't ask her if she had a hat and jersey ready for every team. I don't ask her, or anyone else, anything.

The room sort of spins and I wish I had my headphones on, tune it all out. It's not that I'm ungrateful, I just want a second to let it sink in. Be alone with my own thoughts.

One voice breaks through the noise and I find Gabby standing a few feet away. She's smiling big, genuine happiness written all over her pretty face. I stand and go to her, hug her tightly and lift her in my arms.

Everything else fades away like it always does when she's near.

She doesn't hesitate, even though I'm sure she wants to with the camera following my every move. Instead, she buries her face in my neck. "I'm so happy for you, Zeke. Congratulations."

She pulls back and straightens the hat so it sits right on my head. "Purple and orange are good colors on you."

"I love you." My voice is low, though it's not because I don't want anyone to know. I'm ready to scream it from the rooftops, but the shock of realizing it has stolen the oxygen from my lungs.

"What?" She turns her head as if she didn't hear me, but her eyes are like saucers.

Sara clears her throat behind me, and Gabby pulls away. There are a few posed pictures of me holding up my new jersey and then Sara shoves her phone in my hand and tells me my new coach is waiting to talk to me.

"Congratulations, Zeke," he says, his voice booming through the phone. "Looking forward to having you here in Phoenix with us."

"Me too, sir."

"We've got some temporary housing near the practice facilities until you get settled, but Sara can give you all that information when you get here tomorrow. Tonight, just enjoy."

Tomorrow. It's finally just one day away.

I hand the phone back to Sara and then am met with my friends and teammates, patting my back and congratulating me. Even Coach Daniels made it tonight and he pulls me into a big hug.

"Congratulations, son. It was a privilege to coach you. The Suns are lucky to have you."

"Thanks, Coach."

It feels like hours before I get done talking to everyone and can sneak away to find Gabby. Blair points me in the right direction with no words, just a knowing smile. Vanessa whispers, "She's hiding in the powder room."

There are like eight bathrooms in this mansion, but I start with the closest one. I knock twice. "Gabby?"

"Just a minute. I'm… powdering my nose."

"Let me in, beautiful girl. You don't need powder."

A few seconds later, the bathroom door opens an inch. I push in and find Gabby red-nosed and tears streaming down her face. Alright, so powder wouldn't be totally unreasonable.

"You're crying. What's wrong?"

"I'm just so happy for you." Her cries turn to sobs.

"So these are happy tears then?" I smirk and wipe one away with the pad of my thumb.

She nods, pulling her lips into a tight line and her eyes welling with fresh tears waiting to spill over.

"Liar," I tease and pull her tight against me. With her face buried in my chest, she lets go of the emotions she was holding back, wraps her arms around me, and cries until my shirt is soaked with evidence of her "happy tears."

"I *am* happy for you," she mumbles into me without moving away so the sound is muffled.

"I know you are." I smooth her hair away from her face and tilt her head up. "Tell me why you're crying?"

"Because I'm sad you're leaving." Her face contorts

with her anguish. "Which makes me a horrible person. I'm so happy for you," she repeats for the nine hundredth time. "It's not the same without you here. I miss you so much every single day." She swipes at tears. "God, I'm sorry. We can hang until you leave. Oooh, maybe it'll even make it more exciting trying to cram in a month worth of sex in a few days."

"I leave tonight."

"Tonight? I thought you'd have the weekend at least."

"They want me up there as soon as possible. I was gonna swing by and get my stuff and then head up there, but I could stay tonight, and we could celebrate, just the two of us."

"No, don't be ridiculous. Of course, you should go tonight. Plus, we're sort of at your celebration. Speaking of, we need to get you back out there."

"Gabby?" I reach for her hand to stop her from blowing by me. Once we get back out there in the crowd of our friends, I'm afraid I won't get another chance to talk to her.

When she faces me, I see everything I ever wanted right in front of me. I made one dream come true and all I need for this day to be perfect is her by my side. "Come with me."

"What?"

"There are tons of colleges up there just as good or better than Valley. We can spend every night trying a new position or crossing something off your list, we'll make new lists if that's what you want."

"I think the champagne has made me hallucinate, it sounded like you just asked me to move to Phoenix with you."

"I am in love with you, Gabby. And if the amount of tears springing out of your eyes is any indication, I think you love me too. So, come with me."

"I can't just move with you. I just got here. Valley has been my dream forever and I have the apartment, Blair..."

"Yeah, I know." I shove my hands in my pocket.

"This is silly." She wipes her eyes again. "You're only going to be a couple hours away. It's not like you're moving across the country. We can keep it what it is – casual and fun whenever we have time."

"Gabby," I plead. She knows as well as I do that after tonight, things are going to be different.

She shakes her head and places a finger to my lips. "What we had was amazing and fun and I'll remember it forever, but it was always supposed to end just like this with you getting drafted and continuing to do what you love and me staying in Valley to finally start my life."

The smile she flashes at me seems genuine and I wonder how I got this all wrong. I thought things had changed somewhere along the line, but maybe they just changed for me. Maybe the tears aren't because she loves me. You can be sad someone is leaving without loving them, right?

Gabby came into my life like a wrecking ball and simultaneously tore down everything I believed about what I wanted while inspiring me to want so much more. I got everything I ever wanted tonight, but leaving without her feels bittersweet.

"Let's get you out there, big guy," she says in a playful voice and I follow her without protest."

Gabby

"Gabby, honey, I say this with love, but enough with this movie." Vanessa closes my laptop on the end of the bed and then sniffs the air. "Also, something smells awful in here." She sits next to me and gives me a sad look. "Come here."

Vanessa isn't much of a hugger, so the fact she's offering to hug me only makes me feel worse, but I sit up and lean into her embrace anyway.

"Oh God, it's that shirt you're wearing. Gross, Gabby. You need to shower and change clothes immediately." She pulls back after two small pats. Worst hug ever.

"It smells like Zeke." I lift the neck of the shirt and bring it to my nose.

"It smells like sweaty balls and sadness." She stands

and points. "Shower. Now."

"I don't want to shower his scent off me yet."

She leaves and I grab my laptop and re-start the movie. Maverick and Goose are singing "You've Lost That Lovin' Feelin'" and I can almost hear Zeke singing along. I've been watching this movie for the better part of thirty-six hours.

They've barely gotten to the chorus before there's loud knocking and then Wes and Mario enter. Wes is covering his eyes. "Uhh, sorry Gabby, but we're under strict instructions to get you out of your room."

"She's not naked, man. You don't have to cover your eyes." Mario nudges his arm and Wes drops his hand and then my best friends' boyfriends are staring down at me from the side of my bed with matching guilty expressions.

"It's nothing personal. You understand," Mario says and then he makes the first move, lifting my arm over his shoulder gently and lifting me. Wes gets the other side and I don't even bother fighting because I know their love for their girlfriends outweighs any rebuttal I might offer.

They deposit me in the bathroom and even go so far as to start the shower for me. Then we all stand there awkwardly until they leave and close the door.

With a sigh, I undress and step under the warm spray of water. I miss Zeke and also I'm mad at him. How dare he drop the L-bomb just as he's about to leave. It changes everything. It turns our casual fun into something more serious, and how exactly would that work?

I can't move there, drop my life and go with him.

That's just not the kind of thing rational girls do these days.

When I've used up all the hot water, I get out and pull Zeke's shirt back over my head. It really does stink, but there's just the faintest hint of his scent left, so I keep it on. In my room, Vanessa and Blair have torn off my sheets and are re-making the bed with fresh linens, and I think someone sprayed Febreeze. I grab underwear and shorts and then throw myself on the newly made bed.

"We're going out," Vanessa informs me. "Girl's night."

"I don't feel like it."

"You said you wanted the full college experience. Tonight Phi Kappa Theta is having a slip and slide party. It's as college as it gets."

I search for any bit of excitement, but I can't summon it. "I'd rather stay in and watch a movie or something."

Blair removes a swimsuit and dress from my closet and tosses it on the bed. "You're coming, so get up and get ready."

I send a text to Zeke checking in to see how things are and tell him, for the thousandth time, how happy I am for him. He hasn't responded to any of my texts, which pretty much confirms that I destroyed the possibility of anything happening between us in the future.

Right now isn't our time. Our lives are going in different directions, but someday, after I've finished college and done all the things on my list and he's proven himself in the NBA, then maybe we could have something real.

I feel a teensy bit better once I'm dressed and out the door, but I don't get the same rush of excitement that I did the last time I was at a college party. Turns out a slip and slide party at a frat house is the exact same as it was as a kid. Except back then the boys didn't have six-packs and I saw less boob action from the still mostly flat-chested girls in fourth grade.

We grab drinks and then a seat where we can watch the brave souls taking a run down the slip and slide. Note to self: swimsuits shift into some really inappropriate positions while slipping and sliding.

"This cup stinks," Blair says and looks down into her drink. "And I think it has a floater in it. I'm gonna get a new one."

She heads back to the keg and Vanessa and I watch a girl in a string bikini run and slide boobs first down the yellow tarp. When she stands, one nipple is showing and the bottoms are shoved up her crack like a thong. And of course there's a guy holding his phone up presumably getting the entire thing on video.

"Dirty cups, guys videoing nipple slips, and this beer is warm. College is stupid."

"Bite your tongue." Vanessa turns to me with an appalled frown. "The beer is free, and that girl probably went and asked him to tag her in his Insta story."

I look over and sure enough, she's chatting him up with a big smile.

Vanessa continues, "If you really believed that, you'd be in Phoenix with your hot man. You've just lost sight of what makes college so amazing. It is whatever you make it. If you want to be a sorority girl who's a little bit promiscuous – be it. You want to be the girl who shows her assets at a frat party – more power to you. A jersey chaser who keeps a steady rotation of hot athlete boyfriends – own that shit. Jock, nerd, virgin. You can try all the labels on or none of them. It's about choice. There is no right or wrong, it's just what makes you happy. And I think you let your happy leave without locking that shit down."

"So you're saying I can be the college girl in a long-distance relationship?"

"No, I'm saying you can be the fine as fuck college girlfriend of the hottest new member of the NBA." She knocks her knee against mine. "Or you could bump uglies with that dude wearing a beer belt because he's giving you come-hither eyes."

"I miss Zeke. Why'd I have to waste three years hiding away when I could have been spending them with him?"

"Or you could look at it from the Blair perspective that you got a couple months and that's better than nothing."

Blair plops down beside us. "Okay, first of all – that is so not what I would say to that and secondly… okay, there is no second. That's terribly depressing, V."

"What can I say, I'm a realist."

"So what would you say?" I ask Blair. If anyone can make me feel better, I know it's her.

"I'd say, I've never seen you or Zeke happier than I have the last month and that I think you're great together."

"Okaaay, where's the positive spin?"

"Oh there's no positive spin, there's 'you're an idiot

for not going with him' or at least telling him you're in love with him."

"But you said you were afraid I'd get hurt."

"That was before the man professed his love. You think guys like Zeke just come along every day? Take a look around, my friend." She leans in close and points to a guy a few feet away smashing a beer can on his forehead. "They do not."

Vanessa cackles and throws her head back. "Well shit, I didn't realize we were going with honesty."

"You agree with her?"

"Yeah, pretty much. Zeke is hot, he just signed a multi-million-dollar contract, and he wants to share all that hotness and money with you. It seems like a no-brainer to me."

"I don't care about the money."

"Which is why you're perfect for him. You're not a shallow bitch. He's going to be fending those off with a stick."

A pang of jealousy hits my chest. Fuck, did I screw this up?

"Yes!" they say in unison. Apparently I said that out loud.

"But how would that work? Valley has been my dream forever and Zeke might only be a couple hours away, but he's going to be busy. When would we see each other? How would that work?"

"We can't answer that for you, but don't you at least want to try?"

I do. I really, really do.

"I gotta go." I push my cup toward Blair and stand. I stop when I realize I don't know how I'm going to get to him. "I think I'm gonna need your guys' help."

Zeke

"Getting settled in?" Jason Harris asks as he takes a beer from the six-pack he's carrying and then drops the rest on the counter. Harris was the Suns' second-round pick, coming all the way from Vermont.

He takes a seat on the couch in my new living room. The small furnished apartment is bursting with guys on the team. If the guys in Valley could see me now, they'd die from shock that I'm hosting a party.

"Yeah, I think so." I take a swig of my own beer and glance out at the night skyline. It's only been a few days, but the team have been welcoming and everything has basically been taken care of for me.

Several of my new teammates live in the building. They traded their small furnished one-bedrooms that are standard for new recruits, for larger units upstairs, but the proximity to the training center and the views of downtown are hard to beat.

It's weird without Wes, Joel, and even Nathan. My mom was right, they were like family – are like family.

"What about you? How are you liking Phoenix?"

"The heat is going to take some getting used to," he admits with a shake of his head. "I left a plastic Starbucks cup in my car yesterday and the damn thing was nearly melted when I went back four hours later."

Coming from Illinois, I had the same reaction when I first moved to Valley, but now the heat feels like home.

"You'll get used to it," I offer.

Harris' phone sounds with a text and he shakes his head. "Every girl I've ever kissed has blown up my phone since the draft to reconnect. Ain't that some shit."

Kevin O'Stark, a five-year veteran, laughs. "Being single in the NBA is rough. I suggest you pick one of those and marry her. If she kissed you before you were in the league, then at least you know she isn't just into you because of the money."

Harris nods and points his beer bottle in my direction. "What about you, Zeke? Got a girl you left behind?"

The beer turns sour in my mouth. "Yeah, kind of."

"I get it, you want to keep your options open."

I don't correct his assumption, just nod solemnly. Gabby has texted every day since I left, but I can't bring myself to respond. Each one is so happy and upbeat about the whole situation and I guess I should be glad that she's being so cool about it, but I don't want to be a guy she hooks up with when it's convenient for our schedules. I want to fit everything else in between moments with her.

Maybe when I get a free weekend I can drive down to Valley and tell her that. My throat feels tight and my palms sweat just thinking about the possibility that she might turn me down again.

"Excuse me," I say and head for my bedroom. I close myself in and grab my phone from the nightstand.

I tap out a text to Gabby but then close out before I send it. Another day or two and maybe I'll have the right words. "Maybe I'll grow some balls by then," I mutter to myself before tossing my phone on the bed and heading back out to hang with my teammates.

Harris and O'Stark are setting up the Xbox when I come out.

"You in, Superstar?" O'Stark asks. He's been calling me that since I arrived, but I can handle the ribbing and Lord knows I dished it out to the rookies at Valley.

"You know it, old man." I hold my hand up with a smile and he tosses me a controller.

Gabby

I turn the engine off and press my head against the steering wheel. The reprieve is short-lived as the sweltering heat beats down on the car without the AC running. I double check the address and look up at the tall building across the street.

"This is it," I say to no one.

I grab my phone and purse and walk toward the building. Sweat trickles down my back and I think I might be hyperventilating. Maybe this wasn't a good idea. Perhaps I should go back. All it takes to keep me moving forward is remembering the look on Zeke's face when I told him I wouldn't go with him.

The doorman eyes me suspiciously. I can't blame him; I probably look sketchy all strung out on emotions and sweating profusely.

"Can I help you, miss?"

"I'm visiting a friend. Apartment 303, Zeke Sweets."

I try and look sweet and innocent as he takes me in. "Elevators are to the left." He waves a gloved hand in that direction and I wonder if he's sweating his ass off in his formal uniform of all black from head to toe. I focus on that, on trying to imagine alternate uniforms if I had my own building with doormen, instead of the fact I'm about to come face to face with Zeke.

I've got it narrowed down to all white with a black bow tie or swimsuit attire when the elevator arrives at the third floor. I'm certain my throbbing pulse is visible as I knock on the door.

There's no answer, but I can hear the faint sound of music from inside, so I press my ear to the door in time to hear a laugh that isn't the deep chuckle I know as Zeke's. I'm ready to retreat to my car and call off operation girlfriend when the door flies open.

My gaze travels up to the top of the doorframe and

The Tip-Off

Kevin O'Stark, the Suns' star player and leading scorer, looks down at me with intrigue and confusion. I've done my research on Zeke's new teammates, but now I wish I hadn't because I'd love to be blissfully unaware that I'm standing in front of an NBA All Sar.

"I'm sorry, I think I have the wrong apartment."

O'Stark opens the door wide and calls out, "Yo, Superstar, you got a visitor." Then he extends a hand. "Kevin, nice to meet you."

"Gabby," I say meekly as I shake his giant paw.

"Gabby?" Zeke's surprised voice draws my attention to where he stands in the living room.

I enter the apartment and walk past basically the entire Suns' roster. The room has gone quiet and I can feel their eyes bounce between me and Zeke.

"Hi." I give him a small awkward wave as he crosses the room to meet me.

Some of my nerves fall away as he wraps his arms around me and pulls me tight against him. "What are you doing here?"

"I, uh, made you a playlist."

His hand goes to the back of my head and then smooths down my hair. I hear him chuckle softly. "You came all this way to give me a new playlist?"

"Did she say playlist?" someone asks and then another voice adds, "Speak up, we can't hear you."

Zeke's laughter vibrates against my chest. "Guys, this is Gabby. Gabby, these assholes are my new teammates."

I brave a glance around the room and offer the guys a small smile. "You guys mind if I steal Zeke for a few minutes and, uh, maybe change the music?"

They don't answer, just grin like idiots, until one of the guys unfolds himself from the couch and grabs his phone and the speaker pumping out music. He looks at Zeke with a teasing smile before setting the speaker on the counter. "Speaker name is Harris Jams."

Zeke pulls me by the hand to his room. He closes the door and presses me against it. "God, I missed you," he says just before his mouth descends on mine. His lips are soft but demanding as he kisses me like it's been years instead of a few days.

I pull away just enough to speak. "Wait, I need to tell you something."

"What's that?" he asks and fuses his mouth to mine again.

His mixture of sweet and tender with hard and demanding makes the world stop. It's just me and him and everything else that I thought mattered just doesn't. I told him once that it was the moments spent with other people that mattered and I was right, but the people you give your time to matter more. A million nights with people who only know me from the surface are worth so much less than one night with Zeke who sees me for everything I am and everything I am not.

"What did you want to tell me?"

"Hmmm?" I'm still lost in his kiss when I realize his lips are no longer on mine.

I open my eyes to find his golden browns smiling at my love-drunk face. The words are stuck in my throat, so I pull out my phone and connect to Harris Jams. We sit on the edge of the bed and as Beyoncé starts singing Zeke cocks a brow. "I dig Beyoncé."

The error in my first song selection isn't obvious until

The Tip-Off

I realize Zeke has no idea what I'm trying to say. I skip past "Crazy in Love" and let the next song play. Zeke's head bounces softly to Rihanna, but he's totally clueless.

I press skip again and groan. Blah, blah, blah, Selena, get to the chorus. When she finally gets there, Zeke's expression goes serious and I can almost see the hope building, but he doesn't speak right away. He waits until she's all the way through the chorus a second time before one side of his mouth lifts in a smirk. "You love me like a love song?"

"I'm so sorry I let you leave without telling you. Of course, I love you."

His grin grows wide. "You made me an I Love You playlist?"

My grand gesture is starting to feel like a giant flop. I knew I should have gone with a whipped cream bikini or a tattoo on my vag that says 'Property of Zeke'.

"I don't know how this is going to work, but I want to try because I love you so much. You were not part of the plan, Zeke Sweets."

He laughs. "You either."

There's pounding on the door. "Yo, Superstar, pizza is here."

More voices are crowded around the door, attempting to whisper and failing miserably. "Leave him alone, he's having naked time with his girl."

"Ask him if I can get that Selena Gomez remix. I love her."

"This is not how I would have imagined spending the weekend with you, but my new teammates are as nosey as the last ones, so I don't think they're going away anytime soon." He jabs a thumb to the door.

"It's okay," I say, stand and pull his hand. He stands and wraps his arms around my lower back. "I'm yours until Monday."

He pulls back and narrows his gaze. "Wait a minute, how did you get here?"

"I drove." Just saying the words brings a wave of nausea from the drive up. "Two white-knuckle hours, but I did it because you're worth it."

"Yeah?" He seems genuinely shocked by the sentiment.

"Yes, you and Cliff are totally worth it."

"Uh-uh. Still no to Cliff," he says, pulling me to the door and opening it. He drops a quick kiss to my lips. "But you and he can talk it out after the guys leave."

epilogue

Gabby
Two Months Later

$\mathcal{N}$athan and I circle through the first level of The White House, a mixture of new and old faces. It's the first week of classes and the energy and excitement for a new school year is at peak level.

"Alright, what's your type? Blonde, brunette, redhead? Ooh, how about that girl over there with the pink hair?"

Nathan shakes his head for the billionth time tonight. "What if her natural color is awful, and she goes back to it a month after we're dating?"

"That is strangely insightful." I glance around the room and my eyes fall on a tall blonde with striking features and legs that seem to stretch on forever. "You're making it impossible for me to be a good wing woman being so picky. How about the girl in the yellow dress by the window?"

I move toward her before Nathan can respond. Number one, she's standing by herself and number two she has a look of anticipation mixed with anxiety that tells me she's either new or it's not her usual crowd.

"Hi!" I sidle up next to her, but Nathan approaches her like a rabid coyote. "I'm Gabby. Are you new?"

She nods and turns her drink nervously in both hands. "Maureen."

Nathan is trying his best to hang back, but I loop my arm through his and pull him toward my new friend. "This is Nathan."

"So, Maureen, are you single? Do you think my friend here is cute?"

Nathan chokes on his beer beside me. "Excuse her, too much time sniffing glue as a kid melted her brain."

"Whaaat?"

"You can't ask people things like that," he mutters to me.

Maureen giggles so score one for me and my nosiness. "At least she didn't eat it."

"I like her," I say to Nathan but flash a smile at Maureen.

"And I'm single," she offers and sneaks a quick glance at Nathan.

Score two.

"Where are you living?" Nathan asks, standing a little taller. I pull my arm away so Maureen can step in. My work here is done.

"I'm going to get a drink. Nice to meet you."

Without my partner in crime for the evening, I circle

the party, stopping to say hello to people I know and smiling at people I don't. I don't know if I'll ever be the girl that feels totally comfortable in my skin when I'm in a room full of strangers. Is anyone? But I'm getting there and I'm excited about the semester at Valley and sneaking away on long weekends to see Zeke.

"Yo, Gabby," Joel calls out and I find him staring over the crowd. He nods to the door and I swivel to find my handsome boyfriend walking through it.

He takes my breath away, which is both ridiculous and totally amazing. People watch him, some just stare, others call out or pat his back as he makes his way to me.

"What are you doing here?" I ask as he wraps his arms around me and lifts me, squeezing me so tightly and stealing whatever breath I had left clear out of my lungs.

"I missed you."

"I was going to drive up in the morning."

"I know, I couldn't wait that long. Also, I had an idea." He pulls me behind him out the front door. He stands in front of me, a big smile on his face. "You ready?"

"For what?"

"I was thinking you could drive up in that." He steps to the side and points to the curb. A cherry red convertible is parked at the street. I can almost smell the new car scent, it's so shiny and perfect.

"You didn't?! Oh my God, Zeke, this is too much."

He holds out the key in front of me. "I did warn you I was going to buy you one."

"You're insane."

"Insanely in love."

I roll my eyes, but my heart squeezes. "I love you."

"I love you too."

I grab for the keys and he lifts them high out of reach. "It does come with one condition."

"What's that?" I cross my arms over my chest ready to play hard ball and do whatever it takes to get behind the wheel of that car.

"You let me choose the playlist for the drive."

"You made a new car playlist, didn't you?"

He winks and drops the keys in my hand. "You know it, beautiful."

Zeke

Another Two Months Later

I toss my bag on the floor as I enter the apartment and call out for Gabby. I see signs of her everywhere from her purse on the counter to her backpack lying next to the couch. She managed to arrange her class and work schedule so she only has to be in Valley Tuesday through Thursday, so a good portion of the other days, she spends with me in Phoenix.

My girl is nowhere to be seen though. I head toward the bedroom, pulling my sweaty shirt over my head.

The Tip-Off

Light creeps out of the bottom of the bathroom door.

"I'm home," I announce and peel off my shorts. "Are you getting in the shower? And if so, can I join? My whole body hurts."

"Just a minute," she says and then mutters a string of curses and something drops to the floor.

"Everything okay?" I ask just outside the door.

"Yes. No. Yes. Shit. I'm coming out."

The door opens a crack and she peers out, just her head, blonde wisps framing her face and those ocean eyes sparkling with mischief.

"Whatcha doing?"

"I have a surprise for you."

Intrigued, me and Cliff – fuck, I've got to stop letting her call him that – stand at attention, ready and waiting. She steps out and gravel fills my throat, rendering me speechless. My reaction must please her because she adds a little extra bounce to her step, causing her boobs, which are orange and black, to bounce just like... well basketballs, which is exactly what they're painted to look like.

"What did you do?" I ask when I find my voice.

"I was studying for art class and I decided to use my body as the canvas. Do you like?"

"Very much, except, I'm afraid to touch you." I drop my hands to her hips and slip my thumbs through the string material of her panties.

"Yeah, it doesn't come off very easily." She lifts her hands so I can see her orange palms.

"God, I love you." The girl painted her boobs to look like basketballs. If that's not true love, I don't know what is.

She meets my gaze and smiles, love and trouble written all over her beautiful face. My chest tightens and my heart races. I thought getting to the NBA was the only thing I needed. Basketball was family and success all wrapped up in a leather-bound package. But now I'm looking forward to so much more. Life with Gabby will never be boring, and I need her to remind me that life should be fun and a little crazy. Scratch that, I *want* it and that's so much more powerful than needing it.

"Marry me?"

She goes perfectly still and quiet, my question hanging between us. Slowly, the shocked expression on her face turns to another one of her gigantic smiles. "It's the basketball boobs, right? I knew that was the secret to getting your attention."

"I'm serious." I tug her toward my nightstand and open it, remove the ring box and get down on one knee.

She covers her face with both hands. "Oh my God, you really are serious."

"Will you marry me, Gabby?" I open the box so she can see the ring, but her eyes don't so much as glance down at the round two carat diamond I'm holding. "I promise to love you so damn much. You've made me happier than I've ever been. And, yeah, you do things like paint your boobs to look like basketballs and I wonder how I got so lucky. I don't ever want to stop being surprised by you and your crazy shenanigans. Marry me because before you I thought I couldn't have a relationship and be a great ball player, but now I know that being with you makes me better in every way. Marry me because if it came between you or food, I'd pick you every time."

The Tip-Off

Her smile stretches wider. "You'd die without food."

"Some things are worth dying for."

"Lucky for you, I won't make you choose."

"Is that a yes?"

"Yes, I'll marry you, Zeke. A million times, yes."

the end

Thank you for reading *The Tip-Off!*

Please consider leaving a review!

Coming Soon

Nathan's book is coming Fall 2019! Sign up for my newsletter to be notified of release dates and other book news:

www.subscribepage.com/rebeccajenshaknewsletter

Join my **Facebook Reader Group** for behind the scenes, exclusive excerpts, and more:

http://smarturl.it/RadRomantics

Playlist

- "Put Your Hands Where My Eyes Could See" by Busta Rhymes
- "The Way I Are (Dance With Somebody)" by Bebe Rexha
- "Truth Hurts" by Lizzo
- "I Don't Care" by Ed Sheeran feat. Justin Bieber
- "Young, Wild & Free" by Snoop Dogg feat. Wiz Khalifa & Bruno Mars
- "Whip My Hair" by Willow
- "Bottled Up" by Dinah Jane feat. Ty Dolla $ign and Marc E. Bassy
- "Almost (Sweet Music)" by Hozier
- "Leave Me Alone" by Flipp Dinero
- "My Chick Bad" by Ludacris feat. Nicki Minaj
- "Ruff Ryders' Anthem" by DMX
- "I've Been Waiting" by Lil Peep feat. ILoveMakonnen & Fall Out Boy
- "Ocean Eyes" by Billie Eilish
- "Sucker" by Jonas Brothers
- "Cold Water" by Justin Bieber
- "Beautiful" by Snoop Dogg feat. Pharrell Williams & Uncle Charlie Wilson
- "Beautiful" by Bazzi feat. Camila Cabello
- "Shoot Pass Slam" by Shaquille O'Neal
- "Nobody" by Martin Jensen & James Arthur
- "Nights Like This" by Kehlani feat. Ty Dolla $ign
- "I Got You" by Bebe Rexha
- "Freak N You" by DJ Khaled feat. Lil Wayne & Gunna
- "Here With Me" by Marshmello feat. CHVRCHES
- "Talk" by Khalid

- "Last Hurrah" by Bebe Rexha
- "Issues" by Julia Michaels
- "Blame It On Your Love" by Charli XCX feat. Lizzo
- "Love You Like a Love Song" by Selena Gomez

Also by Rebecca Jenshak

<u>Smart Jocks</u>
The Assist
The Fadeaway

<u>Sweetbriar Lake</u>
Spar
Sweat

<u>Stand-Alones</u>
If Not for Love
Electric Blue Love

About the Author

Rebecca Jenshak is a self-proclaimed margarita addict, college basketball fanatic, and Hallmark channel devotee. A Midwest native transplanted to the desert, she likes being outdoors (drinking on patios) and singing (in the shower) when she isn't writing books about hot guys and the girls who love them.

Be sure not to miss new releases and sales from Rebecca – sign up to receive her newsletter
www.subscribepage.com/rebeccajenshaknewsletter

www.rebeccajenshak.com

Printed in Great Britain
by Amazon